Kennedy's Prayer

Kennedy's Prayer

Kimona

To order additional copies of this book, contact:
Xlibris
844-714-8691
www.Xlibris.com
Orders@Xlibris.com
849700

CONTENTS

Prologue vii

Chapter 1   Saturday - The Jordan Household... Kennedy 1
Chapter 2   Quentin (The Nelson Household - Sunday Morning)....8
Chapter 3   Kennedy 12
Chapter 4   Kaity 18
Chapter 5   Kennedy 21
Chapter 6   Quentin..24
Chapter 7   Quentin..29
Chapter 8   Kennedy 32
Chapter 9   Quentin..37
Chapter 10 Kennedy 40
Chapter 11 Kennedy 42
Chapter 12 Quentin.. 44
Chapter 13 Kennedy 48
Chapter 14 Quentin.. 51
Chapter 15 Kaity 55
Chapter 16 Kennedy 58
Chapter 17 Kaity - Two Weeks Later 63
Chapter 18 Quentin - Two Weeks Later......................................65
Chapter 19 Quentin..67
Chapter 20 Simeon 70
Chapter 21 Quentin - After The Intervention..............................72
Chapter 22 Kennedy 74
Chapter 23 Kennedy 76
Chapter 24 Quentin..78
Chapter 25 Kennedy 80

Chapter 26 Quentin...82
Chapter 27 Kennedy 84
Chapter 28 Lamar...87

Epilogue..93

PROLOGUE

Kennedy- 5 years old

"Mommy I wish I had a grammar or grandpa to stay with when you and daddy get destroyed. I don't wanna stay with Aunt Millie. She doesn't like me."

"It's deployed Kennedy. And your Aunt Millie is excited about you coming. She loves you baby girl."

"Aunt Millie isn't fun. All she wants to do is go to church. She won't let me and Nellie stay up till 10 o' clock on Fridays like you. Mommy, the only nice thing about Aunt Millie is Uncle Greg."

"Well, will you do mommy a favor and stay with Aunt Millie and listen to EVERYTHING she tells you and be a good girl. If you're a good girl, me and daddy will be back quickly."

"Mommy I'm going to pray for a prince like daddy and Uncle Greg to come save me from Aunt Millie and I'm gonna marry him and live with him until you and daddy come home."

"Is that so?" she replies laughing.

"YEP! And he's gonna protect me and buy me snacks and take me out in pretty dresses. Plus you know what? And he's gonna treat me like a princess like daddy and Uncle Greg treat me and Nellie. Plus he's gonna look just like my daddy. He's gonna be tall and muscly and handsome and have a lots of tattoos on his arms and straight teeth and curly hair but he has to have blue eyes."

"Why blue eyes?"

"Fer cause mommy, his eyes have to look like Heaven."

"That's interesting."

"Well Baby, come next to me and get on your knees. And we'll pray that you listen to Aunt Millie and be a good girl until your prince comes and takes you away from her."

That night I prayed with my mom for her and daddy to be safe while they were overseas and mommy let me slip in the prince charming that was supposed to come save me.

Two weeks later, my parents were gone. Killed by enemy fire and I was put into the permanent care of my Aunt Amelia and her husband my Uncle Greg. As I grew up under her iron hand, I'd forgotten the night I prayed for the blue eyed prince coming to save me from her. I guess God heard that part and was getting him ready... It's just that I didn't put a timeline on my hero coming to save me.

CHAPTER 1

SATURDAY - THE JORDAN HOUSEHOLD… KENNEDY

My name is Kennedy Nicole Grant-Jordan. The first lady of Solid Rock Christian Church, Married to the "Right Reverend" Lamar Jordan for the last 10 years with him 14 years on and off since I was a freshman in college. We got married after I graduated college, a simple ceremony since he really wasn't the man I was in love with

I own a clothing boutique, Bella Diva, that services women from size 2 to size 26. I believe that every woman should be given the chance to shine and my outfits, some of which I design myself, range from saved to sexy. Sundays and Mondays are my coveted days off although Sunday's I'm doing the work of the Lord as the first lady.

Lamar and I started casually dating during my freshman year in college and in my senior year, he proposed. My Aunt Amelia (Millie) by this time had accomplished her mission of hooking me up with this soon to be coming pastor. She was obsessed with religious royalty. Often me, my cousin and my uncle suffered her neglect in lieu of her church work. Hooking me up with Lamar was her coup de grace. Lamar decided to start his own church right before I graduated with seven people, which included me, my aunt and uncle, who gathered in the living room of his mother's house. The faithful seven quickly grew into 400 active members and an old synagogue that was purchased right after we got engaged. Today, there are over 1000 names on the church roll, some of them prominent members of the community. And the seven original members hold powerful seats on the official board. I am the first lady, co-pastor and youth liaison. Solid Rock has become Lamar's main source of income because of its miraculous growth and I'd be lying if I said he didn't put his blood sweat and tears into that success. But I'd also be lying if I said that our marriage wasn't a casualty of that work.

My heart, my body, my mental health and my dreams have suffered immensely in order to keep my husband happy and my aunt from stealing my peace as well. I supported him and pushed for success in the ministry, even postponing my dreams of owning Bella Diva until I could convince him that the clothing I sold would be geared toward the women of Solid Rock. Sunday suits, hats and whatnot despite the lingerie and evening wear I designed as well. I also sacrificed an entire relationship in order to satisfy the dreams of Lamar and Aunt Millie.

Monday's are usually mine to regroup, wash clothes. Catch up on my shows, get a massage, a mani/pedi and just chill especially since it's just me and Lamar. After I serve him breakfast, we read his daily scripture that he blasts to the members via social media and text groups we pray and then I send him off to work. Once he's gone, I pull up ANYTHING but the solemn hymns that he insists we play to keep us grounded in the Lord. I even wish he'd play some Kirk Franklin, Jonathan Mc Reynolds or Mali Music but Lamar questions the sincerity of modern gospel music. When he is in this house, it feels like a mausoleum. "*You never know who's watching Kenny. Satan is just waiting to catch us slipping*". When Lamar is around he insists that we always have to be on our P's and Q's. Only hymns, the Christian TV stations and even our reading material must be chaste. *The devil comes to kill, steal and destroy and destroy and we are NOT leaving the door open to make it easier for him.* He knows nothing about my playlist or the cache of romance novels or adult toy collection in the treasure box on my nightstand.

It's Saturday though, and Bella Diva is closed because of some repairs that are taking place due to a storm that hit earlier in the week. Power was knocked out for a few days and some flooding in the basement. My landlord has called me profusely apologizing for the lost day and promising that I'll be up and running by Tuesday. Mr. Rice is a great guy and definitely not a slumlord. If he says Tuesday, he means it with quality work. Since I had the day free, I slept in late. Lamar has an all-day minister's class so he grabbed breakfast at the bagel place on his way. Freeing me from my wifely duties. On my off days, my best friend Teddy, and my cousin Janelle, who is more like a sister, are my hanging buddies if I'm not swamped with church duties.

Since today is an unexpected off day for me, my cousin Janelle is out shopping with her mother-in-law, Momma Shannon, getting ready for my little niece. They're probably getting necessities like pampers and bottles since I pretty much bought everything else on the registry since I'm living vicariously through Nellie. There is nothing I want more than to be a mom but I guess it's not in the cards for me. So I plan on spoiling my niece rotten.

Teddy, texted me last night to let me know she was taking her mom shopping for a wedding dress. Ms. Betty is getting married next month after being widowed for five years. The 60 year old woman met a man who treats her like a super queen because Pop Lanier, was a G. Ms. Betty, decided that her second time around would be a lavish ceremony since her first wedding was over 30 years ago and her finances were nowhere near what they are today. I volunteered to dress the bridesmaids but insisted she go all out on her dress with a big name designer... Not using my shop didn't offend me because she was one of my biggest supporters otherwise.

So today I'm all alone relaxing at home and feeling my inner Tupac and Biggie waging their East coast vs West Coast battle within me. I pull up 90's rap on Pandora, connect it to the speakers and turn the volume all the way up. The Right Rev. Lamar Jordan wouldn't approve of his first lady doing the even Megan Knees in the privacy of our bedroom but here I am twerking in the living room to Pac's, *How Do You Want It*. I got up, showered and went to the kitchen to grab a bite to eat. I decided on hot dogs. Simple right? I made a few hot dogs and french fries in the air fryer, being lazy and not wanting to wash dishes I even ate off paper plates bopping now to Biggie's *Hypnotize.*

In my shop, smooth Jazz and R&B plays as background grown and sexy mood music. The few times he's visited there is always a look of disgust but even the mothers of the church that patronize my shop are in love with the atmosphere at Bella Diva. *"It's too laid back in here and the music allows sin and sinners to run rampant. All that sexual energy."*

Grabbing my food, soda and condiments I made my way to the den just off the kitchen and grabbed one of my novels by my favorite author, Alexandria House. I was just about to get cozy with one of the Mc Clain brothers when my phone started ringing. Since the rest of my crew was out running errands, I knew it had to be my Aunt. I looked at my caller I.D. And sure enough it was her.

"UGH Let's get this over with."

"Hey Auntie."

"Good morning Kennedy."

"Good morning Auntie. What's up?"

"I just called to check on you baby girl."

"I'm good, Auntie. I'm chillin' today, the shop is closed because of the hurricane. There was some flooding and..."

"No!" she interrupted. "That's not what I'm talking about I've been hearing some rumors about your husband and I'm making sure you have your home front secured."

"What are you talking about Auntie? The gossip mill has been quiet since Lanisha couldn't prove her daughter was Lamar's." It sparked up my own insecurities for us to even have the paternity test taken. Lamar was normally distant and judgmental because of his position but lately, he'd been on ten.

"What's going on now?" I was annoyed, frustrated and getting more pissed off at my aunt by the second.

"Nothing specific baby, I just want to remind you that it's your job as that man's wife, to make him happy and keep him happy. And a few babies wouldn't do your relationship any harm either."

I rolled my eyes listening to my aunt. She knew I wasn't happy in my marriage and always insisted that there was something lacking on my part, that I wasn't giving him enough although I served as his co-pastor, personal secretary, maid, chef, chauffeur, valet and concubine while trying to hold down my business, I was at Lamar's beck and call 24/7 yet, somehow my duties as Mrs. First Lady Lamar Jordan LLC were not being fulfilled. This is why I hated answering her calls. Since I was five years old, she treated me well, but always found some way to blame me for whatever was happening.

"You're right Auntie, but there is someone ringing my bell, so I'll call you later." Tired of her antiquated ideas, I was glad to be saved by the bell but wondered who it could be. I eyed the door because the only people who would come visit me at this time had already bowed out for the day with their other obligations. I'm not expecting anyone or anything except sleep and relaxation. Lamar would be gone until well after 6:00pm. "Who the hell could this be?"

The doorbell rang again. "I'm coming!" As I'm walking to the door, I'm trying to remember if I ordered anything because it could be a persistent delivery requiring a signature... I did order an upgrade for my phone but that wasn't scheduled to be here until Monday or Tuesday. Maybe it was early. Since Aunt Millie called before I could turn off the music, I walked to the door bobbing my head to "Who shot ya" by Biggie. I love listening to his music and opted not to pause it because signing for a delivery only took seconds. I grabbed the knob and opened the door to be met with a very beautiful petite woman. She was vaguely familiar to me. "Kennedy Jordan?" Unbeknownst to me the very beautiful light complexion, light brown eyes, sandy blonde bouncy curls, wearing a light flowy yellow sundress, the woman standing at my door is about to drop something heavy on me. Everything she exuded was just carefree and light.

"Yes, how may I help you?"

"My name is Paulette." she sighed. "Paulette Jordan and I have some things you need to see. May I come in?"

Now as righteous and holy as Lamar portrays himself to be, the entire Jordan family is ratchet. When we started dating, I must have physically fought at least three of his cousins because they liked his last girlfriend better. As they got used to me, I was no longer their target. Then it was bailing someone out at least once a week for some form of misdemeanor, usually some form of assault... She didn't look like any of the family I've met in the last ten years but who knows.

I braced myself and allowed the woman to come in. Like I said, her whole aura was light and I didn't feel threatened at all. When I opened the door fully, she had a stroller behind her with a child that looked to be no more than two or three years old. And another child in tow that looked to be five or six years old. I led her to my patio because no room in the house was child friendly since I didn't have any. I offered her and the children something to drink, grabbed a few cups and a pitcher of iced tea that I made earlier. When I sat down, she began to speak.

"I first would like to apologize to you for Lamar having to have this situation come to this." She sighed, shaking her head.

"What does he have to do with anything?" I asked, my curiosity piqued.

She pushed a large manila folder over to me and nodded for me to open it. She continued speaking as I started looking at its contents.

"My name is Paulette Wells-Jordan and I am Lamar's wife. His FIRST wife. And we are still married. Those two" she looked over at his children, "are his babies, AJ is 6 and Amira is 3. When he tells you he is at those all day weekly meetings, guest preaching, or conventions and he doesn't expect you to be there, because of your shop...He's with us." She swallowed, looked me in the eye and continued. "I don't stay in Jersey. He bought us a nice little home just inside of Pennsylvania about forty five minutes from here. I only found out about you a few months ago when I was looking for the kid's birth certificates in his file cabinet. I also ran across pictures of the two of you. I did a little more research and found your marriage certificate and the few more vacation pictures of the both of you."

I listened as I looked through the folder. Paulette Jordan came armed with a marriage and birth certificate listing Lamar Grey Jordan as the husband and father of the three people in my yard. There were professional pictures of a wedding that I was never given the pleasure of having. Although it was in the church, it was between morning and afternoon service and only a handful of Lamar's family showed up. I wore a simple white dress, carried a fake bouquet and Lamar's godfather married us. Quick and painless like it was a shotgun wedding, no reception, no honeymoon nothing that would cause me to look back on the day fondly. More pictures of Lamar with the biggest goofiest smile, proudly holding the two babies in the hospital when I thought he was out doing the work of the Lord out of state. So he has an entire other family, that although they were hidden, he was proud of them. Looking at his wife of thirteen years, his six year old son and three year old daughter had me thinking of my child. We've been married for 10 years with no children because, "in the interest of the ministry we should wait another year". This of course was after my pregnancy in the first year of our marriage, ended with a miscarriage and every year after that he kept pushing my desires to be a mom to the background. By year five, I stopped asking and dove into the ministry. My baby would have been almost ten this year.

Paulette wasn't confrontational, and honestly I saw her as a victim of this man's stupidity as much as I was. Even more so because of the two children involved. I talked with her and found out while we were living in this four bedroom home complete with a yard. Paulette and her children were living in the projects in a 2 bedroom apartment that Lamar graciously paid the rent and utilities. He also promised her something better soon, since she just found out she was pregnant again. He'd be able to swing it since his ministry was flourishing and most of what we had was the product of our joint financial efforts.

I was livid because this over judgmental holy roller deprived me of ten years of my life and ten years of motherhood. *In the interest of the ministry*. I was crying but it was me mourning my wasted years. BUT there was a reason that Paulette seemed so light to me. This was the end of the constricting tunnel with L6th s amar. I finally saw the light I'd been asking God to show me for years.

I asked Paulette to make herself comfortable and not leave as I went into my bedroom, packed some l of my clothes into my suitcase. I pulled up the travel app on my phone and booked one of my favorite hotels by the airport until Tuesday. Hopefully the boutique would be repaired by then and I could stay on the couch in my office until I found something. There was a shower in my office bathroom so I would be uncomfortably comfortable until I could find a place. It wouldn't take me long to find a place since I'd been smart enough to have a rainy day stash. What just happened to me was up there with a category five hurricane though.

I texted Janelle and Teddy to let them know we needed to have a meeting tonight even if it was via FaceTime. "Meeting" was our signal word that something serious had happened and sister time was needed. It was imperative that I speak to my girls tonight especially since, my cousin Janelle's husband, Alvin, was scheduled to preach tomorrow for the church anniversary. Out of obligation I'd be there because I was the chairperson of the committee that invited him. My Aunt Millie emphasized the importance of fulfilling obligations, especially when it concerned the church. More like especially when it concerned Solid Rock.

I knew after speaking with Janelle tonight that both she and her husband would be more than willing to support me tomorrow. Neither liked Lamar and both had been subjected to Aunt Millie's religious tyranny. Alvin has hated my situation as much as if not more than I did. My brother-in-law witnessed Aunt Millie manipulate my relationship with Lamar, causing me to choose him over his big brother Quentin. He and Janelle got to helplessly watch both of us deal with hurting and healing over our love lost.

All packed, well at least until Tuesday morning, I made my way down the stairs with my suitcase when I heard the children yelling.

"DADDY!!!!"

The shock on his face is priceless as he hugs them. He tried his best to hide the WTF moment from his eyes but he couldn't because this was truly a WTF moment.

The way the children were climbing on him as if he were a human jungle gym, made it obvious that he's a pivotal part of their lives and they love him. The way Paulette is looking at him, despite this moment and all its confusion, it's clear that she thinks the sun rises and sets on him. The way I'm looking at the key hook at the front door it's clear that I need to get out of here.

Lamar turns and looks right in my eyes and opens his mouth to lie his way out of this, but his words will fall on deaf ears. The Right Reverend Lamar Gray Jordan had a whole family while at the same time discouraging me from getting pregnant and running my business in the interest of the ministry he led.

"Kennedy! Do you hear me?"

"No I don't. It's more than clear that I no longer need to hear you." Tears were stinging my eyes and I had to get out of here before he was privy to any weakness on my part.

"Lamar, I am leaving tonight. Do not ask where I'm going as it is none of your concern anymore." I continued to talk over his weak explanation. "I realize the importance of being at Solid Rock tomorrow but do not speak my name across the pulpit. Do not speak to me at all. I will smile and shake hands as I am supposed to but it will be my last day serving YOUR people. Tell the church whatever you want because I have no desire to ever come back to you, them or this! There was no need to chase me or look for me because legally, we never were. Romantically, I can't say that ever existed."

"Kennedy? I…"

I turned to Paulette. "I will have my things out of here by the end of the week so that your family can be together." She nodded, still looking like light to me. It must have been the yellow.

I waved my hand indicating the home I made for us over the last decade. Then I looked into the backyard at his children playing in the grass. "Your family needs you." And I walked out with my head held high.

CHAPTER 2

QUENTIN (THE NELSON HOUSEHOLD - SUNDAY MORNING)

"Quentin, you know I don't feel comfortable going to these churches with you. I stick out like a sore thumb."

"Babe, it's been eight years and you know that I'm going to support my brother whenever he goes out to preach. Everybody knows that you're family. There is no reason for you to feel out of place."

"I know but it still feels weird. Like I'm being watched. AND it doesn't help that your ex is the first lady and the one that invited him."

"But it does help that YOU are my wife and the mother of my children and SHE is married to Pastor Jordan for over a decade now. She chose him over me. Besides, she's Janelle's cousin and we barely even speak anymore. Don't you think it would look bad if you weren't on my arm when we walked in there since you're worried about how it looks to others?"

"I guess you're right but as soon as Alvin is done, we grab the boys and hightail it out of there."

"OK, as soon as they give the benediction, we'll leave."

Today, I have been invited to my own version of the twilight zone. I have been summoned by my parents to attend a church anniversary where the woman, Kennedy Grant, now Jordan who crushed my heart serves as the first lady. In the last eleven years, I have only seen or heard snippets of her and that's because her cousin who she grew up with is married to my youngest brother. I met Kenney while she and the preacher-boy were on one of many hiatus. We lasted almost two years while she was in school. In her senior year, although I declared my love for her and she for me, her aunt coerced her into marrying Lamar Jordan, preacher extraordinaire. It took me over a year to open up to a woman and two years later, I met and married Kaity. Kaity is a pretty, 5'6 blonde with blue eyes and a sweet girl. Most of my family thinks I chose her because she reminded me of the woman that gave birth to me. Truth be told, I married her because she was pregnant, we went to Vegas for a weekend and eloped. My dad didn't go for that deadbeat dad shit and I *did* think I was in love too.

Kaity's family was not somewhere I'd want my sons raised. Racist hicks from the deep south that still used Nigger as a part of their regular vocabulary. Imagine her surprise to find out I'm half black but by then she was in love with me and my sex game. My mother, who died when I was little, was a white woman and my father black. I inherited a lot of her features, blue eyes, fine hair, and fair skin. I was what they would have called back in the day, passing. Kaity never mentioned my heritage to her family and when they met me that one time right after we got married, they were none the wiser. I quickly learned that I should keep my mouth shut and stay under the radar to stay safe and possibly alive. When we'd pulled up to her mother's house when Kaity was still pregnant, her cousin was regaling her brothers about his encounter with a coon in town. They found it funny that I thought they were talking about a raccoon. I went there trying to feel them out. "Nah boy we ain't talkin 'bout no animal. This is one of them black fuckers." Kaity nudged me and we went inside once we were shown to our room, I lit into her for putting me in this situation. But the tinge of brown in my skin could easily be passed off as a suntan. Coming up north for college, opened her eyes to a more diverse world which she was cool with especially when it resulted in her six figure salary at a design firm. She got along well with my siblings, nowhere near Kennedy status, but they were cool. Mom and Dad regarded her with caution but still welcomed her into the family.

She didn't grow up in the church and was taken aback at the excitement at the "black church". I was the complete opposite. My dad is the head deacon, my brother Davis and his wife, Juanita, worship leaders and my sister Lainey the church organist. Which leaves my youngest brother Alvin who was recently appointed Pastor of Shiloh Christian church. The Nelson's were and are Shiloh.

According to Al, Kennedy was appointed chairperson of the anniversary committee and having a hard time finding a willing speaker for their afternoon service because Solid Rock had a reputation that preceded them regarding how they attended to their guests. He graciously accepted the invitation as a 'family favor' to Kennedy since he regarded her as a sister. Talking to Al, he was reluctant to go because his mother in law stayed with the drama but he loved Kenney just as much as he loved our little sis Lainey.

"Q, you know I'm only going to that place to support Kenney." Al had been calling me every day this week.

"Du de, but do you really need me there? I know it's been a decade but if her aunt looks at me sideways it's a wrap." That woman and her selfishness completely changed the course of two people's lives.

"That's the exact reason I need the whole family there. I'm not asking the church to support but I am looking for Nelson support."

"Aiight" I conceded, "Me and the fam got your back." He already knew I would be there no matter how reluctantly. I wasn't having our mother ringing my bell and my phone making sure me and my clan made it.

Which leads me to the longest ride ever to Solid Rock. I know seeing Aunt Millie will piss me all the way off. But seeing Kenney will dig up some dormant feelings. Our breakup was unnecessary and extremely painful. I've pretty much avoided both women, for different reasons since that day. This afternoon, I'll have to sit with the family and I'm sure I'll be so close to her that her very essence will invade my senses. Al better not try that 'tell your neighbor or high-five three people mess because it won't be pretty. That's why I'm insisting that Kaity be there with me as an unwelcome distraction. Listening to her tell the boys that as soon as their uncle finishes that they should leave was getting on my last nerve though. She was obsessing over me being so close to the woman who broke my heart. It. Didn't matter that I'd married her and we were almost going on nine years together. Besides, I knew my parents would not allow their grandsons to embarrass them by walking out before the service was over.

We pulled up to the church at the same time as my sister and her family. We greeted each other and I grabbed Kaity's hand as the boys waited outside when they saw my parents pull up. Lainey grabbed my free arm, "breathe big bro". As I headed up the stairs I realized why she was acting as an anchor. At the top in all his pastoral glory, was the man I hated more than anything. The right Reverend Lamar Grey Jordan. Standing at his side looking as beautiful as ever, my love, Kennedy Michelle Grant-Jordan.

CHAPTER 3

KENNEDY

"Kennedy, a proper first lady, is responsible for the flock her husband leads. You owning that boutique is the antithesis of everything I've been teaching so far. The fact that you have gays working there and all that sexual undertoned secular music. And your services promote vanity. Your shop is a breeding ground for sin and sinners. You're going to have to close that shop."

"Lamar? Are you asking me to give up my dream?"

"Your dream does not align with the ministry and there will be issues if you continue to go against my wishes. I will not support you."

"What does that mean?"

"I will advise the members from the pulpit not to support your establishment. You will fall in line with my ministry no matter what. Your commitment is to ME and Solid Rock."

When the Nelson family walked to the door as a unit, Q made it a point not to shake my hand or even look at me. In fact, he kept his hand on his wife's back and pushed her forward to speak for his part of the clan. Alvin's mom, dad, sister and brothers were all present with their spouses, and children. I was happy to see most of them since it had been a few years since I'd seen most of them. I noticed Lamar bristled a little when Pops Curtis pulled me in for a fatherly hug and kiss. My fake smile up until the Nelson family arrived must have brightened even more when my second dad appeared to match his. "Miss you daughter" then holding up a handful of peppermints. It was an old joke between us that while everyone was looking in Momma Shannon's direction that he had the stash and was bribing whichever grandchild was sitting close to him. I was happy to see them all but pissed that Lamar continued to try to touch me so that we would appear to be a happy couple.

I avoided my Aunt most of the morning because I knew she'd have her well-meaning opinions of how I should carry myself today. I'd been getting 'well meaning' looks from her crew since I walked into the sanctuary this morning. I'm honestly at the point where if one more person tells me what I am supposed to do or how I was supposed to react or feel regarding Pastor Lamar Jordan I'm going to punch them in the face and knock the holy hell out of them. These church folk with their well-meaning advice have no idea what their great leader has put me through over the last ten years and in the interest of the ministry. And they definitely do not have any idea of what has happened behind the closed doors of our home. Honestly, there have been many Sundays that I haven't grabbed the mike and belted out my real testimony and today is definitely one of them. Nah! First Lady Jordan is too classy for that. Especially under the watchful glare of the woman who raised me when her sister was killed when she was deployed, my Aunt Amelia. Aunt Millie instilled in me that we NEVER air our dirty laundry in public. Aunt Millie also was the one that insisted that I date and marry this loser, discouraging any other man who showed the tiniest bit of interest. It was Aunt Millie who chased away the one man I without a shadow of a doubt would have made me the happiest woman in the world even today, over a decade later. Because I couldn't extricate myself from her control, listening to Aunt Millie landed me with Lamar Jordan, charlatan, who has made me nothing but miserable for the majority of my adult life. Today, she stood guard as the head of the pastor's aide, sitting where she could keep an eye on me. The church grapevine is full of juice and I couldn't help but wonder as if I were a toddler. Her gaze told me to keep my mouth shut about what happened yesterday, especially in front of the Nelson family. I couldn't help but wonder if one of those old heifers that thought they sat high and looked low for the tea drove Paulette and her children to my house.

If today wasn't the church anniversary to which I committed my time and effort, I'd be at the house packing my stuff and making sure that I was out of that man's presence before he got home from the second service. I'm here though, a fake smile plastered on simply because the guest preacher is my brother-in-law. I was the chairperson for the anniversary committee this year and thought it would be fun to have who I considered friends come by and support us this year. God truly does work in mysterious ways because I'd invited Alvin and Janelle long before this mess happened. Aunt Millie approved of Alvin because he was a "man of God" as she put it. Even though he was less judgmental and stoic than Lamar, once Aunt Millie heard that he felt he'd been called to preach she was on the Alvin Nelson bandwagon. Janelle never got the pressure I got when I was dating Al's brother Quentin because of that. Q was anything but religious at the time. I mean he believed in God but church just wasn't his thing at the time.

So here I am with my big hat on trying to control my face because my thoughts are anything but pure right now. If I could jump up on that pulpit and beat the hell out of that man I would. Janelle and Momma Shannon are sitting to my left as I sat at the end of the pew. Lamar is pleading with me from the pulpit to not say anything. And in the pew behind me sits the entire Nelson family. Q and his clan are sitting at the other end of the pew yet I can feel him. Service is running smoothly and the spirit is high but now it's time for Lamar to introduce the guest preacher. "God is good church!" (Oh boy here he goes) I can't fix my mood amongst the Amens and All the times being echoed at his greeting. I just want him out of my eyesight and earshot.

"It is my task today to introduce our guest preacher. First giving honor to God who is the head of my life. To the most beautiful woman in this church, my wife, my rib, my helpmate First lady Kennedy Jordan…" Whatever he was saying after that fell on deaf ears because I'm ready to snatch the microphone out of the hands of that controlling, lying, cheating no a good son of a… "Lady Jordan, who do I have to fight?" My face must have been belying my feelings because I looked to my left to see Shannon Nelson, the mother of our guest l preacher, had wiggled between my cousin and I, grabbing my hand and smiling. I hugged and kissed her "Hey Ma I'm good" I tried to plaster on my biggest fakest smile but this woman knew me like she gave birth to me. "You're not! But I'm here." She looked at me in that no nonsense tone and kept my hand firmly in hers. "Kennedy! We WILL talk after this" She meant business and I could only answer "Yes Ma'am" as we both turned our attention to the podium where her son Pastor Alvin Nelson was about to deliver the word. I can't lie, she did calm me down to where I could enjoy the rest of the service.

Shannon Nelson, in all actuality, this beautiful woman sitting next to me should be my mother-in-law. Before marrying Lamar, I dated her son Quentin. I loved her son Quentin but out of obligation to my aunt, I was forced to make a decision that broke both of our hearts. She didn't hold it against me that I chose Lamar over Quentin. In fact, during one of the few meet-ups over the last decade, she'd said as much.

"Baby, people are in your life for a reason, a season or a lifetime. You and my baby have completed your season but when you re-unite, it's for a lifetime."

"Ma, you seem so sure of that. He's married, and you know my situation."

"Pshhh!" She waved her hand. "I'm not trying to say anything bad about y'alls marriages but you two WILL end up together and give me a bunch of grandbabies."

I could only shake my head at that. Momma Shannon held on to a hope that her son and I would cross paths again even though I barely interacted with him in YEARS.

The Nelson family supported one another at the opening of a bottle if they had to and today would be no different. So here I am sitting stoically, with my big hat on trying to control my face because my thoughts are anything but pure right now. Having the Nelson clan here couldn't have come at a better time. After service I noticed that Quentin and his little family hightailed it out of there. I was glad and disappointed at the same time. The rest of the crew stuck around waiting for Alvin who pretty much preached a new floor into that building. I was glad to reacquaint myself with the Nelson family. During the time Quentin and I dated, I'd been accepted as one of them. Once I married Lamar, I was kind of floating around on my own. Sure I had the church members but I couldn't relax and be myself with the majority of them.

I knew Aunt Millie would take this entire situation and turn it around where I was to blame. *There must have been something you weren't doing as a wife to please your husband.* Somehow it would be my fault that my "husband" felt the need to have a whole wife and family yet marry me and make me his trophy workhorse. *If you'd only had some children for him...* I was so tired of her 'If only' I knew that at least Momma Shannon knew what was going on because of Janelle. My emergency meeting had her angry with Lamar and her mother because she knew it would be turned around where I was the villain. Being pregnant I knew her mother-in-law would be on standby if anything went down with my trifling aunt. Momma Shannon must have seen the wariness on my face when it looked like my aunt was heading in my direction because she made sure to steer me over to the rest of the Nelson family. Pops, Davis, and Lainey with their spouses and children, preventing Aunt Millie from making me pretend to be that snake's happy wife. Uncle Greg and Pops Curtis had a friendship that started when Janelle and Alvin started dating. So the two dads were planning one of their golf outings as we walked up to the circle.

My uncle knowing what went on yesterday after a two hour conversation was also shielding me. Uncle Greg did and is still doing an awesome job stepping in as my surrogate dad. He made sure that Nelle and I treated one another as sisters. Any competition that Aunt Millie tried to create between us got squashed by him almost immediately. He used to tell me stories about my parents and I knew he loved both of them just as much as he loved me. For someone not related to me by blood, he treated me so much better than my mother's sister. As I got older, it was him I went to with all of my questions. Although he was just as blindsided as I was regarding Lamar, I soaked plenty of his shirts with my tears getting through my hurt with Quentin. Over the years, he'd given me advice about my sham of a marriage and Uncle Greg was the one who secretly loaned me the money to start my business. He saw no reason for me to put my dreams on hold when I'd already sacrificed my heart to make Aunt Millie happy.

When Nell married Al, Pops Curtis took my uncle as a bonus gift. The two of them had everything in common and what started as parents of the bride ended up as a new best friend. At least where my uncle was involved.

I walked up and hugged them all and thanked them for coming, Lainey whispered in my ear. "I have a place you'll love. Call me first thing tomorrow. You can move in on Saturday." I knew she'd never steer me wrong since she was a part of our crew. "Thanks sis." It was all I could say as Alvin joined the group with Lamar smiling like a Cheshire cat putting his hand on my back.

"Well Nelson family! As always Alvin did not disappoint." I have never been so grateful for Al and Nellie's 3 year old who was tugging at my skirt. AJ allowed me to escape from Lamar's slimy grasp as Pops, ever the peacekeeper, answered him.

"Yes Pastor, we are very proud of him. He is truly anointed to bring the word." By this time Aunt Millie came over beaming with pride and hugging Lamar.

"My sons-in-law!!!!" She turned to Lamar, "Son, I know you'll return the blessing when you preach at Shiloh next month. Kennedy and I will be there front and center." I looked at Janelle and her eyes simply told me to play the game, at least today. It gave Lainey a knowing nod. I'd be out of their control sooner than later.

CHAPTER 4

KAITY

For the record, I do not want to be here. I'm pretty much at home at Shiloh at least I can fade into the background there. I'm uncomfortable here for a plethora of reasons but there are two that stick out like a sore thumb Quentin Nelson and Kennedy Jordan. My husband doesn't think I've noticed but ever since we climbed the stairs to the church he's been different. I can tell he is trying to maintain his composure especially since he hasn't been around her in forever. The first time I met her in his presence, I could tell that something was up with those two. She was so at ease in my in-laws home and around everyone except Quentin and he displayed the same behavior. Right now, he's holding my hand and paying attention to his brother's message but his eyes are so focused on the back of Lady Jordan's head that I'm sure he can tell me what he's thinking. I need to get out of here, especially since I feel like the other woman right now. Quentin never looked at me with half as much desire as he's looking at her.

And Mrs. Nelson, yeah I haven't reached the level to call her Momma Shannon after nine years and two grandchildren. She's all hugged up with Kennedy, the two sharing some kind of secret that no one else is privy to. I'm so out of my element sitting here among my "family".

As if God himself was listening to my complaints, I just got a text from my project manager. Lately, I've been working extra hours and I know that infidelity is in the back of Quentin's mind but that's not it. We're trying to land the biggest client in the history of Macellin Decor and if we do, it's a guaranteed promotion with a raise that would double my salary. Whoever said this little girl from the backwoods of Virginia wouldn't make something of herself was drinking the moonshine that my grandpa used to make. I miss my family so much, especially since I'm stuck at this circus right now and my skin color is not the only thing making me feel out of place. As much as I miss my mom and my uncles, there is no way in hell I'd invite them up here to meet the rest of Quentin's family. I'm basically hiding out from them for reasons of life or death. Before I fell hard for him and got pregnant with the twins, I thought I was dating white boy with a tan. The places and people he hung out with when I met him gave no indication that he had black blood running through his veins. By the time I found out that they were his mother's people I was infatuated with him. He never acted like what my family taught me about Black people. In their words, he wasn't a typical nigger. When I got pregnant, I finally met his father and it was late to abort and run, I surrendered and married him anyway knowing that my children would NEVER know my family.

I grew up with a completely racist family with zero tolerance for race mixing. We weren't a part of any organized community, but we carried the same ideologies when it came to white vs black. I came up North with those views but being in a diverse area opened my eyes to some things. I just knew that I wouldn't be able to change the minds of my family.

My phone vibrating again caught Quentin's attention this time. He was finally able to tear his eyes away from Kennedy. "Is that important?" He looked annoyed and I was looking to see if it was another pressing question from the job. It wasn't. It was worse. An unknown number from a Virginia area code. **NIGGER LOVER! YOU'LL PAY!**

Quentin was now holding my hand tighter I'm assuming from the fear in my eyes. My internal jealous tirade was put on the backburner. I had to get out of here for different reasons. I've never been claustrophobic but at this moment, this huge church was suffocating me. My husband was now trying to calm me down, he'd seen the text as well and although he was pissed, he was catering to my torment first. I knew this had to be one of my relatives. My mom wasn't text savvy but my cousins stayed on the internet like it was their job. One of them must have tripped on the live feed of the service and saw Quentin and I, two of the brightest people in the entire sanctuary.

"Al is almost finished. I'm taking you out to get some air. C'mon."

"No, I don't want to get your family involved. I can wait until he's done."

"You sure?"

He was now acting like the man I fell in love with and had babies for in spite of the odds being against us. Quentin was still with me even though First Lady Jordan held a few pieces of his heart in her hand.

As soon as church was over, we high-tailed it out of Solid Rock. We were there to support our brother and although we both had our separate reasons, socializing with the family was not on either of our agendas.

CHAPTER 5

KENNEDY

True to her word, Lainey was on point with the cute little townhouse she found for me. A two bedroom two bathroom with a small patio in the back and a flowerbed in the front for when I'd decided to try to restore my green thumb. The best part is that it is located on the other side of town away from Lamar, his family and everything Solid Rock. My shop is a quick seven minute commute, no different from when I was first lady Jordan but like I said, my girl found me something that was comfortable. Today is moving day but Nelle had booked a spa day for her crew which included Lainey and my best friend Teddy. As always, her and Lainey's sister in law, Juanita was invited but she ended up going with her family to some function for her brother's daughter. So it was the original fantastic four while she convinced me that Al had hired a more than capable moving crew. Lamar and I spoke long enough to agree that this would be the weekend he went to PA and packed his family up while I was removing myself and my belongings from the house we shared. Janelle came over the night before to help me organize and picked me up early this morning so she and I could have breakfast before picking up the rest of the crew.

"OK so let's get this out of the way." After the emergency meeting with her and Teddy, I knew that she'd want some sister time. "Daddy is NOT happy right now." Growing up as sisters, we knew to direct all questions, concerns and comments to my Uncle. "He is too through with that church and your Aunt." Nelle stopped referring to her mother as mom somewhere around her and my wedding. She either called her my father's wife or your aunt. They barely talked and my aunt barely had a relationship with AJ and wasn't gushing over the baby girl that was soon to make her way into the family.

"He is supposed to call me later tonight. It was everything for me to calm him down when I told him what happened..."

"I'm just glad we didn't have to scrape up bail money." We were laughing at how protective he was over both of us. It was no secret that the minute I walked into my aunt and uncle's house at five, that he considered me one of his, even before my parents died.

"Yeah, we just have to keep him calm until my niece is born."

"Oh and I told mommy." She was referring to her mother-in-law. Since her own mother was so caught up in the affairs of Solid Rock, she gravitated to her husband's family. I had too when I was dating Quentin and a lot of times missed our girl talks when we would be at the house.

"WHYYYYY?" I groaned.

"Because she heard me getting pissed off and was afraid that my blood pressure was going to spike up." I nodded in understanding, "Besides, you know she likes to keep tabs on you." I nodded again. We didn't get a chance to talk after service on Sunday, something I was a little relieved about. Uncle Greg and Shannon Nelson were two people who didn't play where I was concerned. The only reason that neither had jumped off the deep end when I married Lamar is because I lied and told them that it was what I wanted. Neither could dispute the fact that Lamar and I had been seeing one another for a long time and maybe there was something they were missing.

"Well, I just hope that this move goes on without a hitch. I don't need the guys Al hired to meet up with Lamar's hurt pride."

"Oh, if he does, that crew can handle it. Especially with Pops in charge."

"Pops? As in Curtis Nelson, Pops?"

"Yeah boo. The Nelson brigade is your moving crew today."

Janelle's father in law, although in his late fifties, was not a weak man. If Lamar stepped to him disrespectfully, he'd tear him to shreds that is if any of his sons didn't get to him first. Quentin, Davis, nor Alvin played when it came to their parents. All three although financially successful, valued family over everything else and had known problem throwing hands to prove it. Knowing Pops would be handling the move, she knew my next question before I could ask.

"Every Nelson male including Quentin and his boys."

CHAPTER 6

QUENTIN

"Aiight Bet, I'll be there at fifteen and Kaity is working this weekend so we have a little extra help. Tell my sis she better be glad I love her. This is my day off."

"Thanks bro. Dad and Davis will be here to help so we can get it done quickly. See ya in a few."

I called my 8 year old twins Jaymes and Jayson in the living room to let them know we were helping their Uncle Alvin move one of his friends to a new house.

"Aw DAD! We are supposed to be relaxing. It's Saturday!" Jayson whined.

"It's for Uncle AJ though. You know he's hooking' y'all up when you're done. Right?"

"He's right Jay. Let's just get it done. Uncle Al pays good even if it's Aunt Janelle's cooking."

Jaymes, the younger of the two, was always the rational one.

When my brother Alvin called me to let me know he needed help moving one of his wife Janelle's friends' stuff, I was all in. For one, I always had my brother's back whether it be minor or major. Whenever he called, I'd come running no question. Second, my sis-in-law had some fine ass friends. None as fine as her cousin Kennedy, but she wasn't available. And hasn't been since my heart was broken watching her accept the proposal from that corny ass preacher dude over a decade ago. 12 years later, and I still avoided her pretty ass at all cost because my heart still hurts for her.

Kennedy was my first real love and truth be told, back then I was ready to wife her. Alvin and Janelle were pushing for the two of us to be together but Nellie's mom was on some other shit and Kenny was devoted to making her aunt happy. Al and Nellie set us up on a date when Preacher boy reneged on a date and there was an extra ticket. After that date, the 2 of us vibed like crazy. I'd pick her up from school to study and chill on a regular. We talked on the phone for hours and she became my best friend that I fell in love with. Preacher boy always had some form of church thing that took his attention away from Kennedy giving me plenty of opportunities to spend real quality time with her. But her aunt decided that she'd be a perfect match for him and when he started his church she'd be a great first lady and so she pushed. To the point that Kenney had to say yes. It didn't help that my brother Davis and I were 6'3 brown haired, blue eyed, tattooed, boys raised by Al's mom and my dad. See, when I was 2, my mom, who was white, passed away after giving birth to my brother Davis. Al's mom Shannon and my mom Arlen were best friends from childhood and she was our godmother. She filled in for my mom. Since Shannon was a single mom with Al who is my age, she moved in with us to fill the role of mom and my dad as Alvin's dad. As luck would have it, the two fell in love, got married and had our sister Lainey. And that is how the Nelson's as we know us came to be. Davis and I have fair skin, dark hair and blue eyes where we could easily pass for white boys especially because of our hair. Alvin and Lainey look like Shannon. The four of us grew up as a family, and you'd better not step to us about the more than obvious differences because hands down, we're family.

As we pulled up to Al and Nelle's place 30 minutes later because I had to bribe the boys with McDonalds, they both were in the back rapping to whatever was playing on the radio. I was lost in my thoughts. Since seeing her in church, Kennedy has been popping up in my dreams. Nothing sexual we'd just be chillin' like we used to back in the day. Our vibe was always off the charts. Like finishing each other's sentences and calling to check on me instinctively, shit like that. I love my wife Kaity, she's a good wife and an even better mom but I never reached that level of love that I had with Kennedy. How do they say, I love her, I'm just not *in love* with her.

Seeing Kenney all prim and proper last Sunday in her 'first lady' outfit, when my brother preached at her husband's church, had me feeling all kinds of emotionally confused. There was a look on her face that I'd never seen before, especially when that clown of a husband stood before the congregation talking about her. That idiot was going on and on about the most beautiful woman in the church and while I couldn't disagree with him on that, I could say her physical beauty paled in comparison to the type of woman she was. And the way she'd straightened up proudly when Ma sat next to her and whispered in her ear, grabbed my interest. Then I saw her smile and kiss my mother. My mind went to a time when we were both happy with one another and extremely carefree. The service had been going on well into an hour and in spite of the celebration, that was the first genuine smile I'd seen from her. She has the most beautiful smile. What happened to it? When she stood up in agreement with the sermon, my eyes focused on her body. When we were together, she had a little baby fat, as she called it, but I loved her curves. Now, she was tight and toned yet still curvy. Honestly, if you'd asked me what my brother preached today…I couldn't tell you. I had to get the hell out of that church when it was over because my libido was in overdrive and it had everything to do with my Kenney. I didn't realize how much I missed her. When she stood with her committee and made presentations, I thought for sure that Kaity would notice my uncomfortable shifting. My thoughts ranged from the simplest to the impure where Kenney was concerned and Kaity was still looking uncomfortable in spite of being surrounded by my family. Right now my wife's insecurities were a turn off and the woman standing in front of the congregation, even though different, had my full attention. After all, we shared almost 3 years of the best relationship of my life. If Kaity hadn't received that text, then I don't think I would have honored her request to leave after the benediction. Even in spite of that text, Kennedy's beautiful everything had my dick so hard that when we got home, Kaity was the lucky recipient of my lust. Even as I sexed my wife, Kennedy Grant's face kept popping up when I closed my eyes. And YES I kept them closed and my mouth shut to prevent me from moaning the wrong woman's name.

"DAD!!! Uncle Al and Uncle Davis are here, and Grandpa too!!!" My boys believed my brothers could do no wrong in their eyes. Besides their grandfather, they were spoiled rotten by the men of the Nelson clan and the women treated them like superstars. They were helping my pregnant sister in law Janelle get into the car with my sister, as if she were going to break. When Janelle popped out this little girl it would be all over. They were already protective big cousins and she hadn't even been born yet. Today it was all the male Nelsons, my father, his 3 sons and our 5, Lainey's little boy included, helping Janelle's friend move. This would be done in no time.

My father and brothers walked up to the car as I was opening the door for my sons. All three had a look I couldn't explain on their faces.

"What's wrong?" I asked because they were just too suspicious for my good.

My dad being the diplomat of the three of us spoke up. "Son, your brother kind of ambushed you today."

"What do you mean pops?"

"It's not that you won't be helping one of Nellie's people move today. It's the person you'll be helping."

"Aw hell, is it that clingy ghetto chick that she tried to fix me up with back in the day."

"No son." he let out a breath, "It's Kennedy." Her name alone was like a brick to my head.

"I'm out." I turned back to the car. "Drop the boys off to me when you're done. I'm not fuckin' wit' chall."

Davis stood behind my truck and my Dad and Al on either side. "Move out of my way. You know I don't deal with her EVER!"

This time Al spoke up. "Q! Nellie promised me that she wouldn't be there at all. As a matter of fact, she was there all day yesterday helping her pack her stuff. Nellie, Lanie and Kenny all went out for the day. Shopping or some shit."

I relaxed a little. A very little. I heard what happened to Kennedy from my mom and Nellie. If her bitch ass fake husband was there I might have knocked his ass out. Like I said Kennedy still held a special place in my heart and hurting her wasn't an option. His punk ass won her over and married her and then treated her like shit. I never liked him and I liked the situation less. But I'm married to Kaity for 9 years now and defending my exes honor would send out all kinds of conflicted messages.

"What about the bitch ass preacher?"

"Kennedy left me the key. He will most likely be with his other family."

"Aiight. Let my sis know I'm only doing this because I love HER! The rest of y'all are some fucked up individuals."

"OK, you're driving." Al laughed as he and Davis hopped in the U-haul and I followed behind with my Dad, my sons and my nephew DJ.

CHAPTER 7

QUENTIN

Moving Kennedy's stuff went pretty much without a hitch. Me, Dad, Al and D carried the heavy stuff while the boys took the light work. When I stepped into the house, I smelled her and had to gather myself because the memories of our love making all those years ago burst to the forefront of my mind. Over a decade and life choice later, she was still my girl.

My sis-in-law was kind enough to tag and label everything we were moving. A few pieces of furniture I remembered she had when she stayed with her aunt, collectible dolls that she'd inherited from her mom. I had to break myself out of walking down memory lane more than once but my brothers pushing to get things finished jarred me back to the present instantly.

"Aye man! I know you're all caught up seeing Kenny's draws but me and Al need to get home to our wives. And I'm sure yours will be waiting for you when you get home." D said loud enough for me, Dad and Al to hear but not the boys.

"Fuck you!" Was the only response I could think of before lifting two boxes and making my way to the U-Haul truck.

It took about 4 hours to get everything out and into her new place and as we were putting the last of her stuff in, Janelle's car pulled up with my sister and Kennedy. I might have been able to ignore their arrival if the boys hadn't run to the car celebrating their aunts' arrival.

"Daddy!!!! It's Aunt Lay and Aunt Nellie. And Ms. Teddy Ms. Kennedy!!!" They should be calling her Aunt Kenny. Aww fuck it. They should be calling her MOM!

Their announcement forced me to look in that direction. My sister was driving with 3 other women in her car. Janelle, Teddy, and my girl. Despite all she was currently experiencing, she looks good. Time was good to her and what was going on did not show in her face... And when our eyes locked, we were having a conversation we both waited almost 12 years to have.

I wanted her, I still love her, I missed her and I could tell, she felt the same. You don't look at someone that way who means nothing to you.

15 years ago-

"Hey, Q. I need you to go on a blind date with me and Janelle tonight."

"What's wrong with her?"

"Nothing man! It's her cousin, Kennedy. Her 'boyfriend' can't make it tonight and I got tickets to this comedy show."

"I'm only going for the show but if she's Janelle's ugly cousin, I'm kicking her ass."

"You're my brother man, I wouldn't do that to you. I'm kind of hoping you two vibe so she can forget all about her boyfriend."

"I'm captain, save an ugly ho tonight then."

"I'm telling you bro. You're going to like what you see."

When we pulled up to Janelle's apartment later that evening, I have to admit my brother was right. I usually gave Janelle the bully brother treatment but when Kennedy walked out with her. All my goofy thoughts went out the window. She was beautiful. Short, thick, big brown eyes and lips I'd planned to kiss before we dropped them off tonight.

"Q, this is my cousin Kennedy." Janelle was all smiles.

"Hi." She was just as nervous as I was. But I heard her whisper to herself "blue eyes".

"Hey, I hope you don't mind me filling in for your man tonight." I couldn't take my eyes off of her.

"No. He's not really into this kind of thing anyway." I'd forgotten all about Al and Nellie in the front seat.

"WHAT!!!??? No smart comments tonight." Janelle saw what was happening and couldn't stop smiling.

"Nah I figure I'll let the comedian do his job and point you out sis." I turned all my attention to the beautiful woman with the large eyes sitting next to me in the back seat of my brother's SUV.

"So Kenney, do you mind if I call you that? Tell me more about your beautiful self." She didn't mind at all and Kenney became the family nickname for the young woman who took total control of my heart from that day on. What was supposed to be a mercy date became one of the realist relationships I'd ever been in. Because I'd already graduated college 2 years ago and was working as a freelance architect, I was able to spend my free time with Kenney. I'd pick her up from school. Take her to my place, fix her dinner, help her study and make love to her until we are exhausted. Because she was still living with her aunt, I had to be patient when she had to cater to her whims which included prancing around preacher boy's ass. My goal was to keep my love happy and let her know she had an alternative to the lifestyle where she felt she couldn't breathe.

CHAPTER 8

KENNEDY

Over 12 years ago I let the one person I truly loved walk away from me and never looked back. Today I'm sitting in his sister's car looking at him like a star struck fan. Time has been good to Quentin. I've heard bits and pieces about him from my cousin over the years. I know he's married, he's the dad of those adorable twin boys whom I met when they were toddlers. None of that matters to me at this moment. This is the first time I've actually seen him this close since I broke his heart and since he ran out of that church like it was on fire last week. I don't count Sunday, since it was my finale in my role as first lady and his wife was clinging to his arm.

I couldn't keep my eyes off of Quentin. To me he looked better than the groom. We were the maid of honor and best man at Alvin and Janelle's wedding. We were both extremely happy for our siblings, they deserved to be together but somewhere during the couple repeating their vows, I got lost in his beautiful blue eyes. My love couldn't take his gaze off of me either and we were having our own private conversation in the midst of the wedding. Just before he'd broken his gaze to present Nelle's ring to Al, he mouthed, "I love you". As part of the wedding party, we were required to do a few dances with Al and Nellie and during one of the perfunctory wedding party dances, Q let me know how he really felt about me.

"Kenney, I never knew that a blind mercy hookup would become my soulmate. I love you and I want you to know that we're going to end up in this hall with Al and Nellie as our people." Since it was a slow jam, we both were obscenely close. And he snuck a few kisses in before he whispered in my ear., "Let's run away after the ceremony and elope. Mamma will be mad but she'll get her chance for our first anniversary" I was all ready to say yes, even to braving the beating we'd get from his mom, when Lamar interrupted and proposed to me. If we could roll back the tape on that day, my Aunt Milly was the one who accepted. Q moved back into the crowd, no one aware of the words he just spoke to me. Confusion all on my face as Lamar slipped the ring on my finger assuming my Aunt spoke for me.

"YES!!! Of course she will OOOHHHH My Kennedy is about to be a preacher's wife. Like Whitney Houston! Both my girls will be married to preachers."

I'll never forget the look on Q's face because I didn't accept the proposal BUT I didn't reject it. Before I realized what was going on, Lamar had swept me up in a hug and people were celebrating. My aunt was the most excited.

Q did attend my wedding which was a few months later, no nonsense why wait. I was hoping against hope that he stood up and claimed me during that object part, he didn't. And I didn't object because it would have embarrassed my aunt and uncle. They'd shelled out a pretty penny to make this day possible. When I said "I do". I saw the back of the most beautiful man in my world stride out of the church and my life. I wanted to chase him like in the movies but I couldn't disappoint my family. After all, Alozno was the right choice according to Aunt Millie.

Things were hard given that my cousin married his brother but for years, he purposely avoided me at the few family functions Lamar allowed me to attend. YES! Allowed. Then he got married. I met his wife, and even attended her baby shower. I bought generic gifts, pampers, plain onesies. I'd just lost mine and Lamar's baby and I was now celebrating the babies of the man that I should be pregnant by. Using my loss as a reason not to stay long and knowing on the inside that I was mourning both my baby and my man. Nellie walked me to my car and hugged me hard. I couldn't put anything past my cousin especially where my heart was concerned. I could feel Quentin's eyes on me that day too but his responsibility was to his wife and his unborn babies. I'd let him go because of responsibility, obligation, after all, Aunt Millie had my best interests at heart. And now I'm in the midst of the mess I allowed my Aunt to cement me in.

When I saw him and his family on Sunday, I'd been going through my own mess. Still am. But it didn't stop me from thinking about him watching me. The few seconds where our eyes met stayed with me until just now. Q had a way of speaking to me without words. His eyes often betrayed his true feelings and although I tried my hardest not to allow it, I saw love last week and now without any distractions, I see the same thing now.

Quentin is still the most beautiful man I've ever laid eyes on. Still in shape and sporting a sexy beard now. I just want to run my hands over his face like he's doing with his own hand right now. He's uncomfortable, it's his tell. He didn't want to see me this close and unguarded any more than I wanted to see him because truth be told, my heart still beats for him. I can't stop looking at him. The music and joking in the car are now drowned out by my heartbeat. He finished his sleeve on both arms. Him being a businessman, he always wanted ink but didn't want it broadcasted I suggested that he get arm sleeves that he could hide when he was in the boardroom and display them in the bedroom. He listened. Back then, he loved the idea and loved it even more when I'd trace the few tats he had on his chest with my tongue. It's sexy… He's sexy. He's wearing a pair of gray joggers and a tank top so HE was evident. I dare not look down. I wanted to run my fingers over every line of ink and every taut muscle in between. I started searching his chest for the butterfly with the K in its wings. The butterfly that matched the one over my heart except mine has a Q hidden in it. I see it peeking from his tank top, right over his heart. His wife? Katy? Kathy? Kaity? Yeah Kaity I knew it started with a K. I hope she doesn't think that's for her.

13 years earlier
"You know my Aunt Millie is going to flip if she sees this tattoo."

"Kenney, if you don't want to we don't have to but this is for you."

We had talked well into the night about getting matching tattoos. I knew my aunt had her own opinions about mine and Q's relationship. She was doing everything to guilt me into being with Lamar.

"Baby girl, this is our commitment to one another. These tats will be on us when we are old and gray holding our great grands. And we'll show them just how long we've loved each other. Even though the 10 kids you're going to have for me is testament enough." *He was holding me against him possessively, one arm around my waist the other around my chest. His lips sucking on the side of my neck this time not leaving a hickey. The tattoo would be staking his claim forever.*

We agreed to get butterflies with our initials in the wings. As well as calling me Kenney, Q also referred to me as his butterfly because with him I burst out of my cocoon, spread my wings and soared. I liked that.

He held my hand as I squeezed it tight, not trying to be a baby when the needle hit my skin. But IT HURT. His hand was red and cramped when it was finished but it was beautiful. I often wondered how I still ended up with Lamar.

"Hi Miss Teddy, Hi Miss Kennedy! His and Davis' boys called out from the front seat of the car. Breaking the trance I was in. Because Lamar kept me away from many Nelson family functions on church business, I never was able to form more than a casual acquaintance with any of the boys except for Nellie's son AJ, even though the Nelsons were another family to me. The twins... could NO! They should be my sons. They looked just like him. Stop it Kennedy. "Hi guys. Thanks for helping me move today. I really appreciate it." I hugged them all, showing a little extra attention to the twins. I gave each of them $10 to go get some ice cream later. It was no secret that I had a soft spot for the twins and they in turn were a little extra affectionate with me. Jaymes acted like his dad but Jayson they say has a mini crush on me. "You're welcome, Ms. Kennedy." They all chimed in as Davis and Mr. Nelson approached the car.

"Hey Kenney, good to see you. It's been a while." They all still used the nickname that Q gave to me a lifetime ago. "You're all set, we're going to head out if you need anything let Al or Nellie know." He put his hand on my shoulder and brought me in for a brotherly hug. Pulling away because I was already a ball of pent up emotions "Thanks for everything guys." I wiped at my now wet cheeks.

This time Mr. Nelson spoke up. "Baby girl, you're still my daughter. THAT never changed. We got your back and have NO problem rolling up on ole boy! We're still your family, especially that pig headed punk over there." He nodded towards the car where Q was now sitting fiddling with his phone looking for something to distract him. Mr. Nelson hugged me and hopped into Quentin's car and they pulled off.

Quentin never spoke to me, verbally, but no one with working eyes could miss the conversation we had without speaking.

"Girl! Not saying I don't like my sis in law but I've NEVER seen my brother look at her that way. You two needed a room just now." Lanie was laughing. "I need a cigarette after THAT." She high fived Teddy as they all walked into my new place. "Girl, I think I got pregnant watching them." Teddy was always so raunchy.

Janelle placed her arm around my shoulder. "He never stopped boo." I knew what she meant but Q is married. And I'm not that woman.

CHAPTER 9

QUENTIN

"Dad, why was Ms. Kennedy looking at you like that?"

"Like what son?"

"I don't know. Like she was just staring at you."

"Not sure son. Not sure."

My father was in the front seat in tears trying to hold in his laughter... Leave it to my son to be so perceptive. Those few moments were the closest I've ever come to Kennedy in years. Whenever Al and Nellie had family functions I made it a point to either hole myself up in their basement watching whatever game was on, or be somewhere with the kids being the fun one in the family. If her husband was there I made my way out because I wanted to throttle the man. Over the years I see she changed. On the outside it looked like Kenney but she became Kennedy Jordan, pastor's wife, church worker. Nothing about her revealed the beautiful woman I knew her to be, My butterfly... Her smile that used to light up the room was a memory. Her laugh was non-existent. Her conversations were dull. She'd become so stoic and serious. She'd even curtailed her sarcasm which back then I found to be refreshing. I remember seeing her in tears at Kaity's baby shower, Nellie holding her as if she was trying to save her. I ignored the feeling that I needed to be there for her instead doing what was right and going to my wife and unborn children. I found out later that she'd miscarried and the baby shower was her first baby related event since. Kennedy was always so strong and forfeited her feelings out of obligation. Preacher boy more than dimmed her light and killed her spirit. And over the years I'd seen her less. At some point in the last decade she disappeared completely, sending her gifts, well wishes and regrets via Nellie or her aunt. Aunt Millie would gush about how perfectly she was filling the role of first lady. I didn't like it then, and now I was so close to her I could have pulled her in my arms and comforted her. Told her she still had a place in my heart. Told her I'd kill that preacher for hurting her, taming her. But I couldn't.

I know my mom wanted me to swoop in at Kennedy's wedding and save her from the fate she was now enduring. Like Al and Nellie, Mom wasn't too crazy about the preacher man or Kaity but she was her grandson's mother... Ken's Aunt kept trying to push the dude in her face too saying he was the 'Next TD Jakes," Mom went to a few services with Millie and wasn't impressed. She outright called him a slithering snake and wanted me to stomp on his head and save her other daughter.

As far as Kaity was concerned, mom didn't hate her but she just didn't think she was in it for me. My dad understood the attraction, said it was something to do with reminding me subconsciously of my mother Arlen. Kaity was a beautiful and decent wife and mother. BUT after being married to mom for almost 20 years, he always said something was missing for us to last.

My siblings, all 3 were just assholes. "Once you go black, you need to go back". And that from Davis' pasty ass. His wife, Juanita was mixed and they'd been going strong for 8 years. My nephew DJ is 6 and Nita is pregnant with a girl. The family is hoping Nita and Nellie go into labor on the same day so we can boast of twin cousins.

After I drop dad off, I have Jaymes, Jayson and DJ for the night. With the Nelsons, it's always family first so the 3 are the best of friends already. Kaity is working late on an account that her job is trying to acquire. She's an interior designer for hotels and large businesses. There's a new hotel being built downtown. Not my architectural work but nice nonetheless. The company she works for is fighting to get the business to work her magic in. I support Kaity but right now my mind keeps floating back to Kennedy. Did she ever make it to the fashion institute? Did she end up opening up that boutique she dreamed about? Did she ever make it to all those haute couture places she'd stay up all night waxing poetic? I can't help but wonder because that sparkle she used to have in those big brown eyes was so dull today.

How much did this man break her down? And what could I do in my current situation to help her heal? I'd have to call Ma but looking at the clock, I knew not to bother her at 10:00 pm on a Saturday night. Kaity was still not home and the boys knocked out, I went into my office, closed the door and turned on my PlayStation.

CHAPTER 10

KENNEDY

I spent the majority of Saturday unpacking and setting things up. I was able to rent a nice townhome on the other side of the city thanks to Lainey's connections. Like the rest of the Nelson clan, she was still a great friend. The only one I'd actually lost was Q. Away from everything that would remotely remind me of Lamar and his trifling band of supporters, My Aunt Millie being one of them. I was too tired Sunday morning to head to church, I didn't have one to go to anyway. With all the time and energy I put into that man and his ministry, I wasn't sure if I'd be attending one anytime soon, maybe ever. Instead I put on some coffee, some smooth R&B and planned to chill today. Maybe do some painting on the canvases I found when I was packing up. I picked up my phone vibrating on the kitchen counter.

PASTOR JORDAN *"Kennedy! We need to talk."*

ME: "Talk to your WIFE and stop texting from the pulpit!"

I blocked his number and poured another cup. After about an hour, I switched the coffee to wine and got into my zone. As I stepped back to look at my work so far, my cell phone rang with a number I didn't recognize. Looking at the time, I knew it wouldn't be my aunt or any of the 'concerned' members of Solid Rock so I answered.

"Hello."

"Hi, is this Kennedy?" It was a female voice on the other end familiar but?

"Yes, it is." I let out a breath and answered cautiously. The last time I graciously allowed a woman in my space, she was my husband's wife.

"Kennedy, this is Momma Shannon. I just wanted to check on you, baby."

Knowing that the voice of the woman on the other end was someone I regarded with the uttermost respect, calmed me.

"Hey, Momma Shannon. I'm OK. Well, as OK as I can be. Just tired today from unpacking and setting up the house yesterday. Would you tell the guys thank you again for me. I really appreciate their help."

"Baby, that's what family does. I know you and Quentin didn't make it but I still regard you as my other daughter. I just called to let you know that if you need anything, especially my shoulder, I'm here. Save my number." To keep the peace in my marriage, I'd changed my number early Lamar's and my relationship and erased all my contacts save for Nellie, Uncle Greg and Teddy.

"Thank you."

"No need for thanks. As a matter of fact, come by around 2:00 this afternoon and grab yourself a hot meal. I know your kitchen isn't completely set up and you could use the company. Lainey, Kaity and Nellie will be here and we can have a girl's pow wow while the men watch the game. Tell Teddy to come by too, and I won't take NO for an answer."

I was a little apprehensive at the mention of Quentin's wife but I was also aware that Momma Shannon didn't play games and would send one of her son's, probably Quentin, to pick me up at 2:10 if I wasn't there at 2:00.

"Yes Ma'am. I'll see you at two." And with that she hung up and I washed my brushes to go shower and get ready for Sunday dinner.

CHAPTER 11

KENNEDY

Sunday dinner at the Nelson's was a staple which included pretty much every member of the Nelson family aunts, uncles, cousins, spouses, and children of all ages. I used to love coming here when I was dating Q. When I dreamed about having a husband that loved me unconditionally and a bunch of children with his pretty blue eyes, my curly brown hair and a mixture of both complexions. Momma Shannon and her sisters always cooked like that was the only meal the family would eat all week. Someone was always bound to take food home and in my younger days, Quentin and I used to argue over who got what. I missed this.

When I married Lamar, I tried to institute that into our home inviting my aunt and some of the mothers in the church but it didn't continue. Lamar was always accepting outside engagements or scheduling meetings after service, where grabbing a quick bite to eat between services became our norm. They were on a first name basis with him at a few of the fast food restaurants by the church. When we did go home he was too tired and wanted to sleep or was so caught up in his "ministry" that we barely had a sandwich together. I also tried to pop in with the Nelson's every once in a while but because of my position at Solid Rock, that didn't last long either. It was awkward being that I was married and Quentin was around but I loved his parents like they were my own. It got harder after my miscarriage to be around all the kids so my infrequent visits became non-existent missing birthdays or anniversaries and citing that I had to attend a church service. By the time Quentin married Kaity, I rarely if ever went to their home. I made my existence known by sending a gift and my well wishes through Janelle.

Teddy and I walked in and were embraced by every Nelson except Quentin. Kaity wasn't there, Quentin stayed on the other side of the room as he always did when we were forced to be in the same vicinity for Al and Nellie's functions.

"Boy if you don't get your ass over here and greet Teddy and Kenney! I didn't teach you to be rude. I swear you are so damned stubborn." Quentin was pissing Poppa Curtid off simply by being standoffish to me. 12 years was a long time to hold a grudge especially since he'd gone on with his life and married and produced those beautiful boys.

"Hey Kenny. I um heard about what happened. Sorry about that."

"Yeah, Hey Q. Um thanks." He gave me an awkward hug almost like we were kids at the 8th grade social or even worse, church…

But I smelled him. I felt him and I wanted more. Of all the hugs I'd received in the last 10 minutes. This was the one I wanted to last. I felt myself relaxing in his embrace and quickly pulled away. From the look on his face, he felt it too. He turned and walked into the living room with the rest of the men and I turned towards the patio with the women. But not before seeing the Cheshire cat grins of the elders of the family. His aunt Coretta didn't know how to whisper quietly to save her life. "Now we just have to get rid of that witch he married." her sisters nodded in approval as I retreated and pretended not to hear her.

CHAPTER 12

QUENTIN

I knew when I saw her last Sunday she still had an effect on me. When I saw her yesterday, I was doomed. And now my mom invited her to Sunday dinner I'm completely fucked. The minute I was forced to be in her space, all my defenses failed. Her perfume was even stronger than whatever I was smelling moving her stuff. Her fragrance changed but it was still Kennedy. Al and Nellie told me the entire story and learned how the preacher boy screwed her over and is still trying to reach out to her. I just want to pull her into my old room and hold her while she cries it all out. We used to be good like that, best friends before anything. Don't get me wrong, we had sex that left us drained and sleeping for hours but we also had a friendship that was second to none. There were things that I knew about Kenney that I would take to my grave and vice versa. In spite of that, she chose her obligation over us and that tore me up. Looking at her on the patio with the ladies, I see it may have done a worse job on her. Face it. She didn't have the support system that I did, especially since her Aunt was the one gunning for her to choose Lamar and her cousin had her own family to manage. Trying to pay attention to the game so I could argue with my cousin because our teams were battling, I repositioned myself in the room where I'd have to strain to see her. I was just about to talk smack when my cell started vibrating in my pocket. I already knew it was Kaity with a sorry excuse.

K: "Not going to make it to Sunday dinner."
ME: "I hope you let Ma know."
K: "Yes. I called. She isn't happy."
ME: "See you at home?"
K: "I'll be late."
ME: "I'll wait."
K: "I'll try."

I understood that Kaity's career was important to her but this family, specifically her sons, were suffering before it. She'd gotten an entry level position immediately after college as an interior designer and worked her way up to where she'd been selected to lead some very lucrative projects. I admired her work ethic. She was determined not to end up back in the trailer park with the rest of her family so she busted her ass. Fortunately, the company she worked for was accommodating when she was pregnant because they valued family over anything else. They didn't make it difficult when she had to take off for doctor appointments or sick days when she was pregnant or with the boys. That's why I thought it strange in the last year or so that she'd begun forfeiting time with me and the boys for projects at work citing tight schedules and deadlines. I didn't think she was cheating. Especially since most of her team was either straight female or gay male but something was preventing her from being a good wife and mother.

My mom was a career woman, in fact she owned her own restaurant. But she held her own even with the added stress of caring for her best friend's children (Davis and I) as well as our own but never shirking her motherly duties. That woman was at all of our games, shows, and teacher's meetings. She was often the one who cared for us when we were sick, occasionally calling her sister or mom to take over. Shannon Nelson was a true superwoman for all four of us. She was a hard example to follow for any woman my brothers and I chose. I tried to cut Kaity some slack in that area but lately, she'd been messing up on every level.

There was the church thing. Like I said, I grew up active in the church and of course I drifted away for a spell. When I moved out of my parents' house, you could count on me to be there Christmas, Easter

and Mother's Day faithfully. Anything else was via Ma's guilt. After
Kenney and I broke up, for a while even the holidays were stretching
it. But right before I married Kaity, I was summoned by my mom for
a service installing my brother as a minister. And at that service, I was
compelled to re-establish my spiritual side. My siblings joke that I went
from demon to deacon in 0.2 seconds. So Kaity feeling uncomfortable
was new because my family made it crystal clear that she was welcomed.

I guess the change started when we made an emergency visit to
butt-crack Virginia when her mom had a massive heart attack. It was
just the two of us given the magnitude of the situation and although I
made my presence known and was supportive. I also allowed her time
with the rest of her family. When we returned home, she was obviously
stressed which I chalked as worrying about her mom. I made it a point
to keep the Nelson boys out of her hair to help her deal with her mom
being sick. Set up spa days for her with Lainey and even bought her an
open ticket to fly back down to butt-crack whenever she needed. But her
attitude changed. She started spending more time at work. She started
missing the boys games, parent teacher conferences, and even our family
game nights. Sex between us was still good but started lacking in the
passion. Whatever happened a few months ago between Kaity and her
family was affecting Kaity daily.

Ma knew of the distance that was growing between Kaity and I
and being the superwoman I knew her to be, she filled in the void by
stepping up in her grandmother role times ten to compensate where the
boys were concerned. That's why right now as she sat down next to me
and grabbed my hand I knew she was about to give me some sage advice.

"Baby, you know that girl still loves you?"

"Ma, HOW?! Kaity is blowing us off again! I know you got her
text."

"Yeah I did. I'm not talking about her fool. I'm talking about
Kennedy."

"Ma, why do I gotta be all that? You do remember that I'm married
right?"

"Baby, you and I both know that this marriage is running its course. And before you were Kennedy's lover, you were her best friend. She needs that right now."

"How? I've barely talked to the woman in over a decade. Not even a hello. If we can avoid one another. We're better off."

"I saw the way you were looking at her last Sunday and your father told me about the nonverbal conversation the two of you had yesterday. So this is how. Seeing that your father is on a beer run and you volunteered to stay with the boys. I'll take my grandsons and send her in here. I can see on her face that she doesn't want to talk about baby showers and weddings right now."

I looked at the woman who has loved me as her own for most of my life and kissed her on the cheek. "I love you Ma."

"You better." She hugged me and walked away calling her grandsons to come help her in the kitchen.

CHAPTER 13

KENNEDY

To say Momma Shannon was plotting from the moment she made the phone call to invite me over would be an understatement. The food as expected is bangin', a typical soul food menu. The seating arrangement was obvious. Everyone is seated next to their S.O. which would have put me and Teddy together but a conveniently unexpected visit from cousin Charles and Kaity's unexpected absence, had me put at Q's right hand which according to Aunt Coretta Zeds where I should be.

Our thighs touch occasionally and my body is reacting as if it agrees with his aunt. Above the table, it is a lot less heated than my core but as much as we both were trying not to, we kept brushing against one another. His pops was sparking heated conversations. Today he was commenting on an article he read about the supposed downfall of the Black family. And although I tried my best to remain composed as I'd been admonished to do over the last 12 years. Lamar didn't like opinionated women so these discussions and debates that were a norm in the Nelson household was a no no in mine. The energy in the room was infectious and I couldn't help myself. I found myself jumping right in, taking the opposing side and using the room we were in as an example. "This here" motioning to the table. "You guys are PROOF that the Black family is still strong. Not one of these children is without their father or mother as an integral part of their life."

Q looked at me smiling. "Yeah Dad, Kenney does have a point. We are the antithesis of that whole argument." Instinctively he put his arm around me only removing it when he noticed the smiles from his siblings and his mom.

After dinner, I escaped to the patio with the women. I was glad because the way I was feeling sitting next to Q at dinner required a cold shower, anointing oil and the prayers of every overweight big breasted, Bible-toting mother in the church. When the conversation shifted to Janelle's baby shower and Lainey's maid of honor duties for their cousin's wedding, I started to zone out. In my current situation, neither appealed to me. I focused enough to answer questions but suggestions were not popping from me as they usually did. Momma Shannon came out and tapped me on the shoulder. "Kenney baby, I need your help with something in the house." I excused myself, thankful to be out of the conversation. I was ecstatic for the individuals but there was so much joy in the room over the same thing that was currently causing me so much pain.

The sneaky old woman walked me into her office and asked me to work on some of her bookkeeping for her on-line jewelry store. I'd been working for about a half an hour when Quentin walked in looking for his mom. "Ma I need..." Oh Kenney, I'm sorry, I'm looking for my mother." He looked as uncomfortable as I felt.

"She went to look for a password I needed. She should be back any minute."

"Do you mind if I wait for her here?"

"No, go right ahead. This is your family's home." I was nervous as hell to be around him. The vibe at dinner. The heat when we accidentally touched. And I wasn't in a good space. I tried my best to ignore his presence by focusing on the computer and Mamma Shannon's numbers. His cologne, something very masculine and very expensive kept wafting in my nose the best way to deal with my senses on overdrive was to ignore him. We sat in silence for what seemed like hours and he finally spoke. He was reading an article in one of her magazines on the table by her couch.

When he finished, thumbing through it, he looked up at me "Kenny, you know Ma isn't coming back any time soon right? It's the set-up."

"Well, I'm done so you can have the room." I stood up to walk out and Quentin stood up with me. Not shocked because his father instilled in him and his brothers how to be true gentlemen. Chivalry was not lost on the Nelson men. What shocked me was when he stood in front of the door, grabbed me by my waist and planted his lips squarely on mine. As angry and offended as I wanted to be, my desire for him overpowered everything. I melted into his arms, my tongue met his and my hands snaked around his muscular neck. My head was screaming to push him away. But I couldn't. Everything else in me wanted this. I missed the feel of his arms around me. I missed his kisses. I missed kissing him back. An involuntary moan and my arms pulling him closer was all the invitation he needed to continue. That kiss, to be kissed like that was something I hadn't gotten during my entire marriage. But it was something that I craved more than anything. I should be feeling guilty. After all, Q is a married man but I wasn't. For all I'd been through in the last 2 weeks... Hell the last 12 years, this right here is where I need to be.

CHAPTER 14

QUENTIN

"Kennedy, I'm sorry. I shouldn't have done that." I pulled away guilty and reluctantly. This was so awkward. "I'm a married man. And you… Damn."

"Yeah Q. You don't have to explain." She is pulling away from me more than physically. The bond between us is still unmistakable even after all these years and I can't deny, I wanted that kiss as much as she was melting into me accepting it.

"Don't do that Kenny. Don't shut down." Back in the day, I could feel her in a crowded room with the lights off. Our relationship was on an entirely different level than liking each other and infatuation.

"I want to help you get through this. And I overstepped just now. I apologize. For that." Even though she tried to break away, I still held her in my arms and instinctively pulled her closer. I couldn't stand to see her hurting. Never could. My mind always went back to seeing her at Kaity's baby shower. That was the one time when I couldn't hold her and ease the pain. And when I realized that I was partially to blame for what she was feeling, I felt like shit.

"Ken, sit down cause I'm not gonna let you go. You need to talk." I guided her to my mom's couch. And the dam broke. All I could do was hold her as she let it all out. I knew Kennedy Grant and this was the first time she let it out since it all went down. She was always the one to put on a strong facade in front of everyone. Especially since she was the first lady of Solid Rock. But right now, at this moment. Quentin and Kennedy were transported to a time when the rest of the world was shut off and she could be herself. I held her tight and let her wet my shirt with her tears. I swear I hear my mom running all kinds of interference outside the door. The boys are looking for me because I promised them a game of touch. Teddy is looking for Kennedi because they came here together. I'm sure my cousin will gladly take Teddy home, they've always had a lust hate relationship and it looked like they were on good terms at dinner.

"I'm sorry, I messed up your shirt." The waterworks finally stopped but we still had some talking to do.

"Forget the shirt Ken, I need to know where your head is right now."

"I can't talk to you. You're biased." she chuckled.

"There must be some reason Ma insisted that we be in this room together. And my marriage. That's another story. Since we're being honest, Kaity is still around because of the boys. But truth be told, her career and those in that circle have become her priority."

"How?! Your sons are adorable."

"Mothering ain't her thing. But what about you?"

"Q." She sighed, "I gave up so much to be with Lamar. I lost friends, family... you." She touched my cheek looking into my eyes... She wouldn't believe if I told her how wrong she was about losing me. If Kenny called me no matter what, I would come running. But she never did. Being a proper first lady took precedence to her needs.

I kissed her palm that was caressing my beard... "Ken, if you haven't realized anything else today is that Shannon and Curtis Nelson did and still do consider you one of theirs. Dad was ready to go to full out war when he heard what happened."

"He was."

"Yeah, he told Al to uninvite him for the service next month. Something along the lines of ripping him a new one."

"Oh really?!" She sunk her body into my embrace and proceeded to tell me all she couldn't tell Miss Millie and although she told them about this past weekend, she wouldn't tell Janelle or her Uncle how much she'd endured in the last twelve years. Kennedy had accepted that she had to deal with so much on her own and I wished that I hadn't distanced myself from her for any amount of time. Me walking out at the wedding was my way of coping but she took it as me closing the door on us.

Somewhere between her story and more tears, I found my lips pressed against hers again at first to comfort her but that quickly turned into more... I couldn't get enough of her. By the time we emerged from my mom's office three or so hours later, Teddy had taken Kenney's car, the boys upstairs knocked out, and everyone else had retreated to their homes. I was now obligated to drive Kenney home. Mom was considerate enough to pack both of us some food and desserts, leaving them on the table right outside of her office. Her note ***Don't fight there's enough for both of you <3*** caused us both to laugh at a long gone memory. My hand never left hers picking up my food, and walking her to the car. When I opened the passenger side for her to get in, she stared into my eyes for a minute before she smiled, reached up to kiss me on the cheek and then slid her perfect body into the seat.

We pulled up to her place about 15 minutes later and because of the hour, I walked her to her door. I was about to run back to my car to take the coldest shower ever when I got home when Kennedy pulled me by the arm, turned me around and lifted her face to mine. I don't know how because I never felt her arms leave my body but I was soon pushing her through her open door and laying her on the couch in the living room What started out as me being a gentleman, a married gentleman, ended up with our tongues, arms, legs, and hearts intertwined with one another.

There were no words spoken. They didn't have to be. We communicated with grunts and moans and of course our eyes. Kennedy's taste was addictive and I'd been clean and sober for the longest time. But once I'd gotten that first taste back in my mom's office, I had to have more. Sucking her hardened nipples into my mouth, my tongue flicking them as they hardened even more and she moaned louder. I found my hand snaking from her full mounds to her extremely wet center. I was so aroused that I found my mouth following my hand to taste her. Kenney's immediate orgasm that coated my tongue let me know that the good pastor didn't know how to savor one of my favorite flavors. Kennedy Nicole GRANT coated my beard a few times and I slurped her up as if I didn't sit down a few hours ago and enjoy my mom and aunt's gourmet meal. She was coming down from yet another orgasm when I stood over her with my rock hard dick. All reasoning about me being married had flown out of the window for both of us. She opened her legs and allowed me to come home. She was so wet and ready for me. And I dove in knowing that there was no turning back. She sucked on my lips, and neck and dug her fingers into my biceps as I stroked her pussy reminding her that I was the ONLY man who knew how to please them both. She was getting louder and thrusting her pelvis to meet my strokes. I hadn't forgotten that it was her tell that another orgasm was on the horizon. This time I came with her, allowing her pussy muscles to squeeze my dick dry. Exhausted I pulled her on top of me kissing her on her lips and then her forehead as I wrapped my arms around her. I just made love to Kennedy as if Lamar, Kaity and years of separation never existed. Our bodies instantly fused together because deep down we knew that we belonged together. "Q. I want this. More than anything. It's not rebound, it's not my hurt, it's a need for you that I've never lost." I kissed her rationalization speech away. Right now, kissing, touching and tasting the woman I never stopped loving is the right thing to do. I ended up in her bedroom making love to her until early in the morning and in between we discussed her pain, her dreams and all that she'd accomplished. Our relationship went to a level even higher than twelve years ago. As I watched Kenny sleep in my arms, I realized that I couldn't go home to my wife because she wasn't home to me anymore. Kenney had never left my system and right here right now it was perfect.

CHAPTER 15

KAITY

I was able to hide my black family for almost a decade. Unfortunately, one of those church social media posts had me found out. That's why momma had her heart attack. I'd muddied the waters by marrying and having babies with a nigger. She'd only half believed me when I told her I didn't know until after we were married. And because the twins looked like slightly darker versions of their father, she'd already denounced herself as a grandmother.

"Your father is turning over in his grave and I'm on my way to mine."

"Mamma, you're being dramatic."

"How did you not know you were marrying a nigger and having race babies?"

"Mamma! Those are your grandsons." I was in tears.

"Don't nothin' kin to me have nigger blood running through it. And YOU!" She looked at me completely disgusted. "You need to fix this before your cousins catch wind and take care of it."

"You can't do anything to them. They're my children!" I was in tears but mamma could care less.

"Let their Nigger daddy and his Nigger family take care of them. Those people are used to welfare and one parent homes."

She could be no further than the truth where the Nelson clan was concerned. They corrected pretty much every stereotype that I'd been brought up to believe about black families, about black people even. But now my family was asking me to make a decision that would probably put my husband and children in jeopardy. I was receiving text messages almost daily, they ranged from taunting and harassment to death threats.

I went home with that heavy on my mind. And no matter what, Quentin did to help me distress, my mother's threat of my cousins coming to take out my children was ever on the forefront. I decided to erase myself from the equation completely. Have Quentin believe that I was cheating or that my job was more important than my family. It hurt that I was missing out on the lives of the twins I carried and bonded with but losing them over stupid bigotry would be a far worse pain than I could bear.

"Kai, we need to talk." Quentin was standing in the doorway looking serious. "What's going on?"

He hadn't made it home last night. I guess my non-committal answer to him waiting up for me had him thinking that I wasn't going to show up. It didn't matter because by the time I got home I assumed that he'd stayed at his parents' house with the boys. He came in with breakfast and the boys this morning making it obvious that he did. "Since we got back from Virginia, you've changed. And the boys are starting to notice it."

Yeah I knew I was watching my babies slip through my fingers but at this cost.

"I'm OK honey, it's just I took on more than I could handle and I'm trying to prove that I can do it in order to get this promotion that's on the table. Things should be back to normal soon." I lied.

Things would become a new normal where I'd be out of the equation. "Kaity, I understand but we need you hon. You not showing up to dinner yesterday caused a lot of raised eyebrows about us."

He didn't like having to make excuses to the boys for my absence and I could see it taking its toll on him right before my eyes. I was willing to lose my family to keep them safe. After that day at church,

I'd stopped letting him see the texts from whatever family member felt like torturing and harassing me. The texts were getting more and more violent and I was sure that Quentin wouldn't hesitate to react. I didn't want him or the boys to even deal with it. I was born into that mess and I would be the one to protect all of us from it.

"Honey, I'm thinking about using that ticket to check on mom in a few weeks though. You'll be okay with the boys? I should be gone for about a week. My Aunt Doris will be coming in from Alabama and I just want to be there to help her get everything situated."

"Sure no problem. But only if you promise to come back and start working on THIS family."

"Yes. I miss my boys. And my man." I grabbed him in a hug knowing that this would be the last few weeks I'd get to enjoy what I'd built. I'd already taken family leave from my job and now that things were cleared with Quentin, I just have to put the wheels in motion to save what I love. I let him make love to me that night and prayed for his forgiveness because this would be our last time.

CHAPTER 16

KENNEDY

It's early Tuesday morning, and I'm in my boutique setting up a new window display. I like to fancy myself on the same level as those during Christmas in New York City. It must be great! Since my biggest opposition was the man that I married, I worked extra hard on my baby. Over the pulpit, not naming me per se, Lamar targeted the shops in that neighborhood by denouncing them as channels to the kingdom. While there were some members who took their businesses to other establishments, his influence was overshadowed by the expertise of the business owners in being skilled in their crafts and producing nothing short of good quality. There was a neo soul vibe in that neighborhood. Pro black, spiritual, prestigious, working people who prided themselves on being the complete package were who we catered to. I was one of many in a mini- mall that housed four other businesses. My boutique, Charmaine's hair salon, is owned by Charmaine Peterson and her two daughters who were the first to grace the mall. Whenever I wasn't sporting braids, Charmaine had a chair ready for me and I came out fierce every time. The Knowledge is a bookstore owned by James and Cassandra Wilson. They are new to the area but have been extremely instrumental in supplying my library of black romance authors. They also seem to have some rare finds that keep me in there whenever I'm on my lunch break. AND Perfect Kutz barber shop owned by six foot seven inches of Simeon Anderson. Simi is a former professional ball player who was obviously business savvy because once he had to 'retire' from an injury, he invested in property all over the area. This mall was one of them. Simi did not hide his interest in me but he respected the sanctity of marriage so he innocently flirted with me but never crossed the line.

The 'hater' vibe that Lamar was perpetrating did not go over well with those who were willing to spend money in our establishments. The whole support Black Business ideology kept us afloat. His declaration to the congregation actually helped my business rather than hurt it. Because it served as more of an advertisement. it also helped that Simi spent the majority of his time at the barbershop, peeking his head into my boutique from time to time to say hi. Simi was one of my biggest supporters, often sending his female clients or the wives / girlfriends of his male clients to support my business. He also hated the way Lamar treated me and made no secret about it. On a few occasions he went so far to embarrass Lamar because he was trying to flaunt his church status. Simi wasn't impressed with his status because he didn't believe that Lamar could back it up with his actions.

"Miss Kennedy, you know whenever you drop that sorry excuse for a man that you married, I'm scooping you up!" This is how every conversation with him started.

"Well Mr. Anderson, it looks like you can throw your hat in the ring. Lamar and I have split."

"AHHHH my heart hurts for you. Get ready my love for me to show you how well you should be treated."

"Is that so?"

"Oh beautiful, you have no idea. Just say the word and paradise is yours."

I blushed and made a mental note to think about taking Simi up on his offer... Even though I'd bared myself completely to Quentin, he was still unavailable.

When I miscarried, Lamar said that my disobedience to him was what caused it. In his words, since I couldn't submit to my husband as far as closing up my shop and forfeiting my dreams for his ministry. Dealing with a married man was definitely on the unforgivable list.

After my miscarriage Lamar refused to impregnate me or even have sex with me, I threw that extra energy into making my shop successful as penance.

This was just one of the things I poured out to Quentin last night and this morning. We sat in his mom's office well past midnight and then in each other's arms in my room; I talked and cried, he listened and comforted me. And although he was a great shoulder to lean on because my old best friend emerged but somewhere in between, so did my old lover. Remember that old R. Kelly song, before his "reputation, *Homie, Lover Friend*? Yeah that was us. And that's how we fell back into rhythm so easily but I couldn't deny that he also had the obstacle of his wife.

It's been 2 weeks since I found out that my 'husband' was a bigamist and I walked out of that house and started my new single woman journey. As expected, he called and texted me non-stop trying to get me to listen to his side. Or maybe he was just trying to see if I was going to press charges so he could finesse himself out of a prison sentence. For whatever reason he needed to call me, I blocked his number. He bought a pre-paid phone and started using that. My notification chime went off for the umpteenth time today and I warily checked it.

Finally, I received a text this morning that had me grinning from ear to ear.

Q-Good morning beautiful.
Me-Good morning.
Q-Just want you to know I am thinking about you today (and that kiss)
Me-I should feel bad about it but…I don't.
Q-No. It's been a long time coming annnnd. We'll talk later. :-x

Q dropped by a few times to check on me and although we didn't have sex again, we did end our visits with his lips on mine. I was reminiscing about his lips in la la land when I heard the door chime. Looking at the clock, it was 8:45, Mrs. Harris, the head of the missionary board, had an appointment at 9:00 this morning, and I was waiting for her to spill the tea as to what Lamar told the church in regards to me leaving him and Solid Rock. She is always one of my first customers knew I would be there early to make sure everything is up to par as far as the customer service that I valued. She was also one of the few members who I could call to minister me through the situation rather than gossip. Once I got settled, I called Missionary Harris.

"Hey Baby, just so you know, I've been missing you at service, Bible study, and prayer meeting."

Yes, even when I thought he was out spreading the gospel, I was faithful to the ministry more for my own salvation than anything else.

"I know momma, but I'll be looking for another place of worship now."

"I hope so. Don't let this setback lead you down the wrong road. Baby. I'm liable to meet you wherever you go. That ministry will be blessed to have you."

"Well that will be a little way down the road."

"I don't know. Word is you've been hanging with Pastor Nelson's family lately."

"Mother, you do know that Janelle is married to Pastor Nelson? I'm just spending some quality time with my cousin before she has my goddaughter."

"You're right but don't think I didn't notice his brother watching your every move during the anniversary."

"His brothers are married."

"Well the one with that white girl on his arm looked like he was ready to ditch her for you if you said the word."

Quentin's eyes. If you weren't paying attention or weren't familiar with him, he had the best poker face. But his eyes revealed everything he was feeling. I saw him watching me, and made note of it too. Since Mother Harris knew everything about Lamar, and wasn't too keen on how Aunt Millie manipulated me into the situation. I figured I'd tell her about Quentin and how I was forced to let him go. She often spoke about being unequally yoked when Lamar and I were in her presence and I knew she'd picked up on Quentin's and my feelings for one another. She was one of the ones I could talk to. Although I didn't tell her everything, she helped to function under the stresses that Lamar provided. By the time I'd gotten to all that went on last night at his parent's house, she was fanning herself.

"Child, I knew it! That boy's eyes never left you. Jesus Himself could have tapped him on the shoulder and asked him to move over and that boy wouldn't have noticed a thing!" Both of us were laughing to the point of tears.

"Again Mother, we're just friends besides, he's married."

"I'm not for breaking up relationships baby, but don't be surprised if by this time next year, you're legitimately changing your last name."

I sobered up with her declaration. After spending time with best friend Quentin, last night, there was a flicker of hope that lover Quentin would soon follow.

CHAPTER 17

KAITY - TWO WEEKS LATER

I've been out here in the sticks with my mom for two weeks now. I miss my boys, all three of them, but I have a lot to do down here to keep them safe. I get to sneak away and talk to them for a bit every day and I cherish that time to hear about their day and tell them how much I miss them. I never want my boys to think that I don't love them. Jaymes keeps asking if he can come be with me. And there is nothing I'd love more except of the twins, he's the darker complexioned. His presence would stir up the hornet's nest for sure.

Ma and Aunt Doris have me serving as their personal errand girls today so I'm out in my Uncle's pickup truck running in what seems like the entire state, picking up medicine, food, and stuff to make these ladies extremely comfortable. Honestly, I've driven a few counties over and I've been out all morning. Looking at the clock on the dashboard its almost two and time to check in with my boys. "I'm just going to pull into the Wal-Mart lot up the road and make this call." The shopping center is only a few miles up the road and I figure while I'm in there I can pick up a few house dresses and slippers for Momma too. I missed my turn though because my cousin's pickup truck pulls up beside honking and both of them yelling out the window. Thinking nothing of it because both of them have loved to challenge me to a race since I first got my driver's license when I was fourteen, I step on my gas, flip them the bird and make my way down the two lane high way opting to go to the store tomorrow. I just want to get somewhere and call my husband and sons to let them know I should be home by next week. Laughing at my cousins I turn up the radio and focus on the road ahead of me until I feel a jolt from the back. I look back not only to see my cousin's monster truck is the one that rammed me but they're holding their hunting rifles out of the window "They play too much." But when they ram me again, the look on their faces tell me this isn't one of their macho games. I pick up my phone to dial Quentin and let him and the boys know that no matter what happens, I love them. But before I can swipe to their contact, I feel one more hit that pushes me off the road and flips over a few times. All I hear is metal crunching and glass breaking as I hit my head pretty hard on the window and the airbag releases. My head is pounding, vision is blurry and blood is everywhere. Everything below my waist is trapped under crushed metal so I can't move. "Help." I cry out hoping that my cousin was just being a jerk on the road and is coming to my rescue. After all we grew up together more like siblings. I feel a little relieved when I hear footsteps. He's coming to help me. I hear my cousin's voice and cry out to him, "Help me Nicky" through my blurry vision I can make out his figure. But then I hear him, a sinister laugh. "This is what you deserve for fucking with them niggers." A gunshot as the car goes up in flames and everything goes black...

CHAPTER 18

QUENTIN - TWO WEEKS LATER

"Ma, I've been trying for over two hours to reach Kaity and getting nothing. I'm starting to get worried. She was supposed to check in around two and it's eight now. No calls, texts, nothing..."

"Did you call her mother, baby?"

"Yeahhh about that." Kaity had been gone for two weeks now. And somewhere between day three and five. I found out exactly what her mother thought of me and her half breed grandsons. Despite that, Kaity found a few minutes every day to and speak to the boys even if it was just a simple text so they wouldn't hear their grandmother's ramblings. We'd also talked about separation and divorce. It was more than evident that we'd fallen out of love and were pretty much co-existing for the sake of our sons.

I hinted to my mom about us breaking up because she'd become the head cheerleader and coach for Team Kennedy. BUT I didn't have the heart to tell my mom about Kaity's mother. Mainly because I knew she'd be going off much the way she is right now since I was forced to tell her. "...They don't need those types of people in their lives anyhow. And when they make it big and are billionaires, those racist bastards bet' not shift their eyes in MY grandsons' direction. They got some damned nerve!" She was fuming and cussing so bad that my dad heard her over the lawn mower outside and came in worried. Everyone knew it would have to be the devil himself standing in front of my mother to get her as riled up as she is right now. Exactly why I said nothing until I was forced to. Which is why right now I'm trying to calm both my parents down. When my phone rings. An unknown number but a Virginia area code.

"Hello."

"Good evening, this is the Brodnax Virginia police department. We are looking for Mr. Quentin Nelson."

"This is he, Is my wife OK?"

"Sir, we're calling to inform you that Mrs. Nelson was involved in a fatal accident. Her car was run off the highway by a drunk driver and the injuries she sustained were fatal."

My parents seeing that I was about to pass out from on my face ended their ranting. My father grabbed the phone and spoke with the officers while my mother made me sit down and grabbed a glass of water for me. Before I could blink, all my siblings and their spouses were at my side. Davis and Nita took the boys, Alvin and Janelle had travel and lodging arranged, Lainey was on the phone with the coroner and I was numb.

CHAPTER 19

QUENTIN

Because Kaity had 'tainted' the family lineage by dealing with my family, her mother wanted nothing to do with her body. Alvin flew down to Virginia with me to collect her and she was laid to rest a week after I received that phone call. The boys were devastated but thankfully they had their cousins to buffer some of their hurt. I wasn't sure of how to feel because we were talking about going our separate ways. I hadn't reached out to Kennedy since that day I found out Kaity died, even though she was at both the wake and the funeral service. I saw her but didn't acknowledge her presence. She didn't push through. I'd received a few texts from her just checking up on me and I ignored them. I felt like I was doing a disservice to the memory of my wife by entertaining my ex. That ex specifically. I'd cheated on Kaity with Kennedy and had to have pushed her away to her death. My guilt forced me to fall into a routine of sorts, keeping an eye on my sons, making sure they were getting through this hump in the road without disrupting their lives more than it has been.

It's Friday and the boys are out again with whichever member of my family picked them up. They'd be gone until Tuesday evening since Monday was a holiday and I'm sure my mom or whomever had them would get them to school. I was alone in the house and thoroughly enjoying an entire bottle of whiskey while watching the game. Or rather letting the game watch me while I went through yet another bottle of whiskey. The last few months, this has become my weekend norm. Friday and most of Saturday, I escaped to the wonderful world of whiskey. The biggest decision was whether to do it in the privacy of my own home or catching a ride share to the dive bar a few blocks down the road. Since sober Q had every intention of watching the game tonight. I figured I'd go hook up with some horny MILF at the bar tomorrow. If I played my cards right, I'd end up having her get me off in the bathroom, her car or she'd spring for a room at the short stay by the airport.

I'd become a shell of the man I was and what messed with me was that it wasn't over Kaity. I knew that relationship was over long before we agreed to split. But I felt like a complete asshole because I was plotting on how to capture Kennedy's heart while I was still a married man. The guilt over that and the fear that in the face of death, I was worried about losing the one woman whose very essence vibed with mine. Because of that, I let her go. The stuff Kennedy was going through, she needed someone who could be a constant shoulder to her. I needed to be that person for my boys. So in the course of six months, her phone calls and texts went radio silent. She hadn't been to any family dinners in a while. Because Kaity was no longer here, I was exempt from attending Janelle's and Juanita's baby showers. My sisters-in-love understood what I was going through and didn't push. Since the funeral, I'd successfully resumed avoiding Kennedy at all costs. I couldn't be her hero or her demon slayer when I was battling with my own.

The game was almost over when I was awakened by my cell ringing and banging on the door. I knew it had to be one of three people. Dad, Davis or Alvin. Opening the door to all three, "What in the intervention do you guys want?"

"Exactly", my dad said pushing past me so that he and my brothers could enter my home. They all took a seat on the couch tossing the blanket I had draped over me into the recliner I was now forced to sit in.

"How can I help you guys?"

Alvin spoke up this time, "We have appointed ourselves the Don't be a dick and lose the best thing that ever came your way again committee."

"The WHAT?!"

"My brother. We understand that you lost your wife, physically, but honestly you'd lost Kaity long before that. It has however come to our understanding via Brother Alvin, an extremely reliable source, that the one woman that has total reign in your heart, has been fixed up and is seeing someone OTHER than you for the last 4 months. They were tag teaming me now."

"Yeah man, since you essentially ghosted her, and she understood to a fault, she was fixed up with a very nice young man. Everything Aunt Millie would approve of. He even has Momma's interest piqued."

"Well if that's the case, I wish her well." I said as I took a swig from the bottle this time. I deserved to lose Kennedy again at this point. That night she gave me her heart and her body to take care of once again in spite of Kaity and I failed...

"No big brother, that is not the proper response. We do not wish her well because THAT would mean that the two of you are settling."

"Yo. She deserves someone better than me. Maybe it's time we let go of the what ifs of the past. Dad, Al you are men of God. Maybe this man is her ram in the bush. Kennedy deserves to be happy and I'm not the one." With that I turned to watch the tv and took another swig of my almost empty bottle of whiskey. They all looked at each other defeated.

I had allowed her to walk away from me once again. Well at least I could focus on my kids and give them my undivided attention.

CHAPTER 20

SIMEON

I have tons of money. A billionaire by all accounts, and while most people thought I'd been savvy with my earnings playing pro ball, few knew that as a young 'un I was heavy in the streets. Smart enough to stack, but cunning enough not to get caught. In college, I was 'that dude' kind of like little Tariq on that show *Power*. There was always a suspicion but never enough evidence to pin anything on me and I continued to stack. A lot of those players you heard about on the news fucking up their careers and their lives with drugs and shit. That was me. The money was real good and they kept it coming. The malls, apartments and shit was just my way of cleaning shit up. Most of my barbershop clientele was in there for more than a haircut. For most of my conquests, money talked. For Kennedy, it wasn't speaking her language though. You won't believe how happy I was when I found out that the little preacher boy messed up. You see, although I was feeling Kennedy, I had other reasons for her to be on my arm. She was the perfect person to help clean up my image and maybe get the feds to turn their heads in another direction. Suspected kingpin dates and marries the first lady. I was even considering buying a church and turning my life over to God, or at least making it look like that. I had been working on her for so long, I didn't see any reason to prolong this thing when she decided to accept my offer to date me. I went in full steam playing the love struck smitten role. It wasn't hard because well Kennedy was fine. I'd noticed that the first day she opened her shop. And I'd finally be able to tap that regularly.

We've been dating for six months, seriously for four and I've caught wind that the eyes that were on me are starting to pull back because of my new woman and the acquaintances I've made since becoming "serious" about her. My plan is working flawlessly. Tonight we're supposed to attend some birthday party for one of her friends and I think I'll shake things up by proposing to her. When the word gets out that I wooed and wedded a church girl and a legitimate business woman, All eyes OFF me. Tonight I'll pour out my heart and then slip a giant rock on her finger. I hope she likes it; I was able to get it for a steal.

CHAPTER 21

QUENTIN - AFTER THE INTERVENTION

To say the Nelson intervention helped me get my head out of my ass would be giving all of them the permission to gloat. BUT it did. Let's face it. Kaity and my relationship was over well before she traveled to VA. I don't deny that she loved me or the boys and seeing the reaction of her family to us and her corpse spoke volumes to what she was doing to protect us. I loved her for that if for nothing else. But life does go on. When Davis called me to tell me that the man Kennedy started dating was Simeon Anderson, I sobered up quickly. I wasn't a street nigga by anyone's definition. Curtis and Shannon Nelson made sure of that but the name Simeon Anderson meant more to me and my brothers than just a pro ball player. That name held a lot of weight in the streets. He was bad news when he was in junior high school with us and only became worse as we grew into men.

"Davis, did you tell Dad?" My father was a retired cop, one of the reasons all four of us stayed on the straight and narrow.

"Yeah, He said he's going to handle it from his end but you need to get Kennedy out of that mess."

"Will there ever be a time when I'm not protecting her?"

"Yeah when she has your last name. Then we all will."

I hung up with Davis and called my dad. It seems he's known for a little while about Simeon Anderson and was already in touch with a few of his friends in high places. Janelle's dad. The very quiet unassuming Uncle Greg turned out to be a retired FBI agent. They couldn't go into details but after making a few calls to old friends they discovered that Simeon Anderson has been on their radar for a while now. Dad also let me know that Janelle's mother also orchestrated this hook up with Kennedy from behind the scenes. Apparently, since she couldn't hold on to a preacher, maybe she could land a rich thug. He was tired of seeing his niece being used as a pawn and while working on saving her from this heartbreak, he was also filing for divorce from his conniving wife

CHAPTER 22

KENNEDY

Tonight I'd be attending a surprise birthday party for Lainey at some banquet hall. The dress code, grown and sexy. And looking in the mirror right now I fit the criteria, especially the sexy part. The dress I wore was one of my designs, a one shoulder body hugging dress in my favorite color, fuchsia. All my accessories were silver since that was one of my favorite color combinations.

I'd maintained my relationship with the Nelson family but only reduced my role to family friend especially after Q's wife died. I tried to maintain our relationship knowing that he had to be strong for his boys. I was willing to be strong for him. I thought after the night we shared in his mom's office that we were going to open a new chapter. Boy was I wrong. I ended up cutting all ties after Kaity's funeral. The looks I received from him for being there as his friend were just short of deadly. Q could always control his body language but as always his eyes betrayed him every time. I saw that whatever he was going through he regretted what happened between us and his guilt consumed him. In less than 3 months I allowed two different men to attack my self-esteem and I wasn't going to give another woman's son to have that power over me ever again. Heartbroken again but at least this time, I walked away with my pride.

Catching wind of my singleness, I was approached by Simeon Anderson shortly after I'd made my decision to cut my ties with Q. Simi owned the barbershop housed in the same mall as my boutique. He's had his eye on me since I opened my shop years ago, but respected that I was "married". Simi would always refer his client's women to my store for their clothes and these women weren't afraid to drop a few dollars for my merchandise. Some even commissioned me for originals.

We have been dating now for four months and I can honestly say Simi is EVERYTHING that Lamar tried to be and a few things that Q is. I have a lot of fun with him and he enjoys spoiling me in spite of my protests.

"How else am I supposed to show you I'm feeling you if I don't try to give you the world." I'm happy and hopeful.

Tonight Simi is my escort to Lainey's party. Showing up to my door with a bouquet of 3 dozen roses white for hope, pink for friendship and red for... love? I let him in so I can put them in some water. When I came out of the kitchen Simi was on his knee with one more long stemmed red rose, the signature black velvet box and hopeful eyes.

"Kennedy, you know now that we've only been dating a few months but you have been in my heart since I met you years ago. You are a beautiful woman destined for greatness and I'd be honored to take that ride with you if you'll have me."

While my heart didn't do flip flops when I saw him like it did whenever I was around Q. I do care about Simi deeply. Once the initial shock wore off. I found myself nodding.

"Sweetheart, is that a yes?"

"Yes. YES. I'll marry you."

I found myself genuinely excited about the future I was about to embark on. Kissing him deeply we had to break away reluctantly before we missed the birthday party. At the celebration, I would be sporting a Harry Winston marquise diamond.

CHAPTER 23

KENNEDY

I am floating on cloud nine as we enter the venue for Lainey's party. Simi and I were late for obvious reasons that I couldn't wait to share with the crew. I see the crew and their significant others were all in place. Janell, Alvin, Teddy, Tyree, Davis and Juanita. There were four spaces left open two for Semi and I and two for Quentin and whomever he was bringing as his plus one. Since I was back in rotation with Janelle and Lainey, I was privy to Q' s private life. He'd taken Kaity's death hard because of the racial backlash from her family. On top of the boys losing their mother, they also lost their family on Kaity's side. They in no way want anything to do with her children. I was willing to put in the effort to support him and his children but my texts and visits were ignored which opened the door for Simi. Of course my girls were pleading with me to be patient with Q because let's face it. Nobody loves me like he does but his situation was too stressful to rekindle a relationship. And I felt like he'd told me to fuck off for real this time around.

"Hey Y'all!" I said while I waved my new jewelry so that my girls could see.

"HEY...OH MY GOD!!!!! Kennedy is THAT an engagement ring?!!!!"

Simi, who was all smiles, kissed me in the cheek and answered, "Yes I asked her to marry me and she accepted."

Janelle and Teddy gushed. Q's siblings offered their congratulations but it didn't seem genuine. I noticed... Simi didn't.

While we were accepting our accolades and getting situated, Q walked up to the table with his date. A short dark skinned girl with very little of her original packaging. Fake hair, nails, lashes, boobs and booty on his arm. If she turns the wrong way something is going to fall off of her. Why am I jealous!

"Wassup family! What are we celebrating before the celebration?" He'd already given me a once over and I could see he disapproved of Simi in his eyes. I was suddenly afraid of his reaction and looked to my girls for help. Davis spoke up.

"Hey Bro. Looks like Kenney got engaged."

"No shit?"

"Yeah."

"Well this calls for a toast."

I don't know who looked more shocked, me or his brothers. Q was taking this surprisingly well. Or that's what we thought until his toast began.

CHAPTER 24

QUENTIN

"Everyone lift your glasses to Kenney and Simi, I'd like to make a toast."

I could see D, Al and Ty eyeing me suspiciously. After their intervention, I'd been talking to them and my dad about winning her back. I was aware that she was dating the barber that owned the shop in the same mall as her boutique. But he threw me for a loop proposing to her. Which meant that I was going to have to move a little quicker than I planned. It sucks because Lainey and Demetrius helped me out and she considered it a part of her birthday gift. I was glad to see them walk in and asked everyone to wait until she arrived at our table. Giving Lainey a nod, she hurried her greetings and they made their way to our table. Ma and pops following behind.

I saw the jealousy in Kennedy's eyes when I walked in with Aisha* the Barbie doll. I almost blew my cover because I was so over seeing her hurting. Despite her obvious infatuation with this joker, that look said it all. I still had her heart. That made what I was about to say even easier.

"Looks like tonight is a turning into a milestone celebration for the Nelson family. My baby sister turning 30, my brothers becoming new fathers, and me finally capturing the heart of my love."

Kennedy looked horrified. "YOU CAN'T BE SERIOUS!" Her eyes moved back and forth between me and Aisha. Simi who was looking flustered and agitated since I walked in spoke up nervously, "Congratulations."

"Thank you Simi, and I'd like to apologize to you for what I'm fuck up." I turned to Kennedy, took her hand out of Simi's and held it on my own. Her eyes were intent on me and not noticing how her girls including Ma had gathered around her and the men had formed a protective circle around us.

"Baby, you cannot marry this man. I know that I've screwed up our second chance but they say a third time is a charm. I'm hoping that after this. We can take this next journey together." I motioned for Aisha to come with the manila folder she had tucked away in her purse. She handed it to Kennedy and I pulled up a chair for both of us and stuck by her and let her take everything in.

CHAPTER 25

KENNEDY

By the time I finished reading the folder, I was glad about three things.

1. That plastic black Barbie was not Q's newest conquest.
2. I hadn't made any tangible wedding plans.
3. I was the love that Q was speaking of.

Plastic Barbie was actually Special Agent Aisha Blake of the FBI. Simeon was being investigated for money laundering and as it turns out he was a top player in the game. He used his barbershop as a cover to move his products which also included some of the young women he suggested use my shop for lingerie. After reading a few pages and not being able to go any further. I took my ring off and was even more shocked when Agent Blake asked to have it as evidence. Turns out the ring was stolen from the wife of one of his rivals with her finger attached.

"WOW I just have the worst luck when it comes to love." My head was in my hands trying to will myself not to cry. I'd done enough of that for everyone in the room. But I felt my hands being pulled into my lap and kisses being peppered on my face. Those same strong hands lifted me from the chair and embraced me.

"Your shirt."

"Woman! Damn my shirt."

"Q!" I began laughing through my tears.

"So Kenney? Third times a charm right?"

"Only if it's with you."

"Kenney?"

"Yes."

"Marry me right now."

"Q! Are you serious!? How?"

"Al is willing and able. You have your two closest friends right next to you and my dad will gladly stand in as your father. A small intimate ceremony. Right here, right now and I can take you home and make love to you until the sun rises."

"OK."

Within minutes, Lainey's birthday party was turned into a mini wedding ceremony. The only person missing was Aunt Millie. Because she was babysitting Lamar's children while his wife was in labor. Ironic right. It was while Uncle Greg was walking me down the makeshift aisle with flowers created from the centerpieces. The deejay hired for the party downloaded the wedding march and we made our vows. When it came time for the rings I was about to freak out when Uncle G pulled out the most beautiful masculine gold band with a row of diamonds for me to slip on Q's finger. But the shock of my life came when Q pulled out a ring that I used to eye in the jewelry store over a decade ago.

Even though we'd said our vows, he eyed Al and began speaking.

"Kenney, about 13 years ago we stood in the middle of the dance floor at Alvin and Janelle's wedding and I whispered in your ear how I felt about you. Do you remember?" I nodded my head.

"Well, my nerves got in the way but I had every intention of doing what the preacher boy beat we went to the mall. I bought it hoping that you'd give the US one last try."

I was in tears as were pretty much everyone in the room that believed in our love.

"I now present you Mr. and Mrs. We should have been married by now. Nelson."

Kissing among cheers and applause. I realized that the prayers of a 5 year old had finally been answered. Down to the blue eyes.

CHAPTER 26

QUENTIN

Today is Alvin's pastoral anniversary. Lamar is slated to preach today and I am on edge... Al decided not to cancel because it would be petty. Fortunately for us though, their former first lady was my better half (finally) who brought her love for the ministry and a few members with her when she joined her family's church.

We just got back from our family moon to Disney. Kenney thought it would be a great idea to get to know the boys at the happiest place on earth. The three of them bonded so fast and they were calling her Ma in no time. Jayson took to her like I took to my mother. I know Shannon Nson did not give birth to me but she would go through the fire for me and I would do the same for her. I saw that same loyalty in my youngest twin's eyes. I also found out that Kenney used to spoil the boys a little extra when she was around them. She told me that she'd only treated them like they could be hers because if it weren't for her aunt, they would be.

"Kenney Baby, are you ok? Cause we can skip this one if you aren't." I was more nervous about Lamar speaking this aft aren't. Then she was. I already let her and my brother know that if he said one word out of pocket, I would go in his mouth to him where not even ma could stop it.

"Baby stop worrying. I am not sweating that man or my aunt. Lucky he's not a long winded preacher and we can come home and get back to work on baby girl Nelson." She was straddling me as I sat on the bed kissing me all over my face and neck.

"Ewww you two are so gross. Mommy, I need help with the iron." Jayson was pulling my beautiful bride away from the kiss that would have made us late or not go to church this afternoon.

We stepped into the church at the same time as her aunt who was carrying that man's new baby as if it were her grandchild. "I'm ok" my grip on her hand had tightened. I was pissed off at her. She kissed my cheek, "I'm going to go speak to the few that did show up. You save me a seat." Aunt Millie acknowledged her actual grandchildren but she was already distracted by Lamar and Paulette's babies vying for attention that AJ left her and climbed up Uncle Greg who had already taken Jessenia, Al and Janelle's new baby.

My mom hadn't sat down yet I saw she had her eyes trained on her daughters (Janelle and Kennedy). She would tear the church up along with me if Millie got out of line and seeing the way she disregarded her grandchildren for that man's babies. My baby was always strong but getting from under the tyrannical thumb of her Aunt, sparked a whole new fire. The minute she said "I do" I saw the fire in her eyes that she had 13 years ago.

My dad and Uncle Greg were rounding up the grandkids since service was about to start. Where Aunt Millie didn't acknowledge my boys, Uncle Greg was the complete opposite. At our ceremony, he let the family know that he was proud to have a double connection with such a loving family. And that the boys would be blessed to have another set of grandparents. Unfortunately, it turned out that he only spoke for himself but his presence in their lives since that day spoke volumes.

I grabbed whatever children that the grandads couldn't and made our way to our seats. Kennedy and Ma sat down shortly after.

"I love you Quentin Nelson. Thank you for being my prince charming."

CHAPTER 27

KENNEDY

It was past time for me to deal with my aunt and my ex-husband. Both of them had manipulated me to the point where I almost lost the man and the family that loved me unconditionally. Then to almost have me marry a known king pin, yeah Aunt Millie had her hand in that too. I found out that even though Uncle Greg was one of the greatest men I knew, my Aunt settled for him because she had a crush on my dad.

My parents dying gave her the opportunity to control my life even down to who I should date and marry. I also found out that the night me and my mom prayed for my prince charming, my mom called her sister just to laugh at me. Aunt Millie recognized Quentin as that man, down to the blue eyes. If she had to settle, then her sister's daughter would never get the man of her dreams either. I'd also found out that Uncle Greg was tired of her shenanigans and after trying to knowingly marry me off to a known drug pusher he left her and filed for divorce. Uncle Greg had been my supporter since I moved in with them at 5 years old. I couldn't ask for a better extra dad, well except for Pops Nelson. He taught both Janelle and I that finding a Prince Charming wasn't a fairy tale. Funny how we ended up with Nelson brothers. An easy win. He was one of the losses that Solid Rock suffered when he moved his membership to Shiloh to be close to his daughters and grandchildren.

I made my way over to Aunt Millie who was sitting with Paulette and holding the new baby possessively. She was and still is Lamar's biggest fan. I don't know why but she was willing to be a mom and grandmom to his children more than her own.

"Hey Auntie, welcome to Shiloh."

"Hi Kennedy, did you see Pastor Jordan's new baby? Aliyah is his third..." She held up the baby so I could get a good look. She was pretty but I wasn't going to be pulled into the petty. I turned to Paulette. Like that day at the house, I had no ill will toward her. "Congratulations on the new baby. She's beautiful."

"Thank you. And I hear congratulations are in order." She grabbed my hand looking at my 10 carat pink diamond engagement ring with the matching platinum wedding band. Eyeing it wistfully. I knew the bastard she married was cheap and would never splurge on something like a piece of jewelry even though she pushed out three of his big headed babies.

"Yes. I am so blessed and my man and my family are such a handful." As if on cue, Jayson who was trying to escape his father and his grandfathers was at my side grabbing my waist in a hug. "Mommy, it's time to go sit down at church. C'mon before they get me." he started pulling on my arm. Jay was so protective of me and I guess he sensed that I was in the lion's den because he was adamant about me leaving. Q noticed and made his way over to us, picking up Jayson but not leaving my side.

"Sweetheart, both of your grandpas are boo-loving with Jessie. And I thought you were going to sit with AJ." I made a point of specifically mentioning Janelle's babies. But Aunt Millie's response was classic. While she noticed them and greeted them earlier, Lamar's babies served as a distraction and were obviously more important. Aunt Millie scoffed. "Taking care of some other women's babies without any of your own. This marriage is doomed."

I noticed my mother-in-law out of the corner of my eye and knew she was ready to pounce. It's bad enough you attack me and Q. but her grandbabies are NOT to be touched. As much as I hated my aunt for how she treated me, I still was raised to treat my elders with respect but before Momma S could get to Aunt Amelia, Mother Harris was in her face.

"Now Amelia Parsons, I haven't watched you try to break Kennedy down for too long. And what you are NOT going to do is come in here flaunting Pastor Jordan's family around like it's something she should be ashamed of. The way I see it, the way anyone with two eyes sees it. Both Kennedy and Janelle have made a come up of miraculous proportions. And with no help from you. They are blessed to have men that love them to the end of the world and show it, children that want to be with them and a REAL family that supports them. It would do you some good to open your eyes and realize that your head has been in your ah…"

"Charlene!!!" My uncle cut her off before she could be struck by lightning. When he decided to leave Solid Rock, Mother Harris was waiting for him at Shiloh. The two had always been friends with me and my wellbeing as their common bond. But with the changes, she became the unofficial soon to be official 'other' grandmother. Mother Harris grabbed his hand and they walked over to their seats. With Jessenia and Jaymes in tow.

CHAPTER 28

LAMAR

As long as I've been a preacher, I have never been this nervous, ever. I heard a little raucous out there between Trustee Parsons and Mother Harris. I even saw the way that Paulette was coveting Kennedy's rings but both she and Kennedy knew that wasn't my style. Today I will make things right. Yes, I married Kennedy knowing that I already had a wife but it was because of her aunt's continuous nagging.

At first it was my job that would take me away where I would be spending with my real family. I was a jerk to Kennedy because I wanted her to get so pissed off that she would leave. Her miscarriage was at my hand. I'd been slipping a chemical into her juice that would induce premature labor and it worked. I didn't want her to have any ties to me when she was able to break free from her aunt's control. I feel guilty about taking a life like that. It's part of the reason I do not approach the subject of abortion in my sermons. But it is also something I'll take to my grave. I needed to free both Kennedy and myself from Amelia when the time was right.

That woman was crazy then and even more so now. She became obsessed with Kennedy's unhappiness and the church's reputation. Not for saving souls either. Oh, don't get me wrong, Amelia Parsons played the role of a "T". You would think that she was on fire for the work of the Lord but from where I stood I knew firsthand how cold and black her heart really is.

Kennedy was genuine but I didn't love her. We got along as friends but that was it. I knew the way she was with Quentin. He was her everything. And she was that for him too. I made sure that our churches had a friendly relationship but I disappeared and then he returned to the church when his brother was mad pastor with a wife and a set of twins. I knew her cousin had told her about them but seeing g her witness his family that should have been hers fueled NY guilt even more. Kennedy would never break up a family. That was evident by the way she packed up and walked out of the house that the two of us built never looking back

I had a word from the Lord to bring to the people but confusion was running rampant through. The church and sadly it was my member that was causing it.

To say that Amelia Parsons had her hand in a lot of the things that went wrong in my life was an understatement. I was happy with Paulette and my children but she insisted that Kennedy would help the ministry grow. And it did. At first it seemed like her ideas were valid but when she kept pushing me to have children with Kennedy I took her miscarriage as a sign from God. When she went against my wishes (actually Millie's) and start her business at another sign. And when Paulette showed up at my door and Kennedy simply walked away from me without a production that was it for me. I just wanted to come clean about all the drama I was a puppet of.

Even now, I allow Millie to dote on my children even though hers are running around the church being showered with love from both their families and the members. I wanted that for my family, for my church. Somewhere my vision got clouded by power and prestige. AMELIA.

"I know that I stand before you this evening and some of you are wondering why did I even bother to show up. Well it's because some things are better off doing face to face. Paulette will you come up to the front. Kennedy AND her husband as well."

I took a sip of water as the three cautiously me their way up front. Both Paulette and Kennedy knew I had a flair for the dramatic so they were eyeing me and each other. I saw Nelson man standing all over the congregation including Pastor Al. It was a sign to me to not try anything slick. I even noticed some of the women coming out of their shoes.

"Good. For you former members of Solid Rock, I ask you to stand as well."

"Church my name is Lamar Grey Jordan, I am a man and I am a sinner. If you find yourself standing before me today, it means that my actions have somehow affected you immensely. I played with some of your lives selfishly, thinking only of my personal gain.

To my darling wife, you have stood by me despite the confusion. When you found out about my double life you could have left me high and dry but you didn't and I love you more because of that.

Kennedy. Listen! Solid Rock, run back and tell everyone that this woman here endured so much and gained so little married to me. I was being governed by someone else's agenda and I'd like to apologize. First lady here left because of MY indiscretions.

And I treated you as if you were insignificant and your dreams and aspirations did not matter. My worst sin against you was removing you from a man that truly loved you. And well. What God has b put together let no man put asunder. It's amazing how after all these years I can still see where this man loves you and I apologize for attempting to break up what couldn't be broken. She dreamt about you man. Called out to you in her sleep. I pray that both of your lives are abundant. Flanked by her husband. Kennedy actually accepted the olive branch I was offering."

The only person stewing was sister Amelia and after the tngu laying she received from Mother Hare is I'm surprised she hadn't tucked an d run. I'd had. Long galleries with Paulette about allowing her to use our children to display her hate. It served us no purpose. Monday, we started interviews for a live in nanny to give my wife a little help. What was coming next was something I'd spoken with Alvin brother to brother about. It was part of the reason he acted like he couldn't cancel my appointment with Shiloh.

"Shiloh and Solid Rock neither I nor Pastor Nelson have been completely honest with you. We didn't cancel this appointment because there us a healing that needs to happen. Shiloh I've started it by baring my guilt to your current and former first lady BUT There is a common denominator that has been an underlying force in all of our lives. You may call vanity or greed or any one of the 7 deadly sins that dam I nate your life. But I'd be wrong if I didn't call out this person in the midst of both church and family."

I noticed that Paulette had now grabbed Aliyah and was sitting closer to some of the mothers from Solid Rock. My children were now sitting with the Nelson children. Quentin was holding his wife protectively and possessively. And Alvin with his wife were standing by my side. His right arm around her comforting her, his left hand on my shoulder.

"SISTER AMELIA PARSONS. If we all were to stand before the microphone today and give our testimony, there would be one common demonization to all of our tests and trials. YOU. Under the cloak of ministry, you have manipulated and messed up the lives of almost everyone in this room. Your own grandchildren do not recognize you yet you are giving the attention they deserve to my children and for the life if me, I do not understand. But it is not my cross to bear. You have hurt more than you have helped based on your own hateful agenda. And as God himself banished Lucifer from heaven, you are banished from Solid Rock and the lives of the Jordan's, Parsons and the Nelsons."

I could say no more because she jumped up eyes dark and crazy. Looking between Janelle and Kennedy she started yelling. "Both of you whores have done nothing but ruin my life. Because of your mother I have always had to settle for less that I know I deserved. But I fixed it when she died. I was given the chance to have the life I wanted through you and you being forced on me as a child I was able to get back at her for taking the life I should have had. As for you Janelle, you were the anchor that tied me down to your father. I have never loved him and the life he gave me was mediocre at best."

But before she could say anything else Shannon Nelson knocked her out. "Charlene I'm glad you got your chance earlier because that felt GOOD. She had it coming for years."

EPILOGUE

Kennedy.

Since Alvin's anniversary which we found out was a set up to put my Aunt in her place, things had changed drastically. Lamar and Paulette, became a pivotal part of mine and Q's lives. They asked us to be Aliyah's godparents to which I was hesitant but Q. He saw it as a way of building a bridge, so I complied. It turned out to be a good decision. We are now at Aliyah's first birthday party which happened to be at our home. And the gang's all here. It took only a few weeks before Janelle and Lainey decided to offer the olive branch to Paulette and make her a part of our crew. It turned out to be an extra blessing because she could burn in the kitchen so most of our girl's nights revolved around her trying out new dishes. The first time I entered that house was awkward but Paulette spared no expense making me feel comfortable. By the end of the night I was drunk and loving everyone. Including Lamar who heard me singing some Keyshia Cole song.

I found out that Al canceled the anniversary service for all other outsiders so only those considered family to him and Lamar were in attendance. The two of them had talked so long about what went on between the churches and the families, they deemed it necessary for us to confront the issue head on and begin healing. He had already re-scheduled an actual service two weeks later where Lamar was a respected guest and given the opportunity to hear one of his and Alvin's mentors. The two of them were like kids in a candy store and Janelle, Paulette and I could only laugh at them.

Q and I are still honeymooning. He took just me to Hawaii for more of a bae-cation. And I guess that's when we created our twins. This time it's a girl and a boy who we decided to name after my mom and dad. I love that although not his first, my first babies are the product of such strong love. I was head over heels in love with my family, my men. About 2 months into our marriage, Jaymes and Jayson sat us down for a serious conversation. While they loved their mother dearly, they asked if I could adopt them and be their official mother since Grandpa Greg and Auntie Janelle were their family they wanted it on paper. I was worried that their infatuation with me would die down or they'd feel like they were disrespecting Kaity but here we are at 1 year married and my sons still go hard for me. I guess Q and Davis were a great example with Momma Shannon.

Soon after I married Q, I dropped the Shannon. Between her and Mother Harris, now Parsons, I had all the mothers I needed. And that punch... raising 3 big strong men, there was no question she knew how to throw hands when necessary. It took all three of them to get her off my aunt that day. She was fed up because she knew that woman had her hand in all the misery that her sons went through regarding the women they loved. My aunt tried to press charges but they were dropped when the entire congregation from both churches were willing to testify that Aunt Millie provoked her. Besides since losing my uncle and the support of the church, her finances dwindled down to nothing. She'd almost lost the house we grew up in but ended up having my uncle buy her out and leaving to a destination unknown. Not that any of us cared anyway. Uncle G and his new wife moved in the house because there was plenty of room for grandkids *and* the pool that Janelle and I begged him to put in when we were 8.

Q is on the grill for this party. My man; looking more delicious than those burgers he's making. I was already a horny mess with my husband because of how sexy he was to me but this pregnancy had me going from zero to one-hundred in less than sixty seconds. He couldn't get enough of my swollen belly which made him just as horny as I was, if not more. That is except when he was talking to them. Which I often woke up to him doing.

"Hey, you got a girl cause I'm feeling you."

"Yeah, sorry and she's about 14 months pregnant about to drop my twins."

"REALLY! 14 months!!"

"I love you. Kenney." He was laughing as I hit him. I was over there to distract his attention enough to snatch a few delicious kisses. Of course it worked.

"I love you back Q. And is that burger right there ready cause your babies are hungry."

"Woman! Go sit down and I'm sure one of your cackling biddies will bring you something."

"Fine."

I went to sit down with my mothers and sisters but not before I saw the sweetest thing when Aliyah toddled over to Quentin, "Daddy Coo". and he just gushed all over her. Q was destined to be a girl dad. And this little one growing inside of me was about to be spoiled with a T... spoilt. Between her older brothers, her dad, her cousins and her uncles I felt sorry for anyone that even had a thought that she was cute. Jessenia was already the apple of their eye and she was only a few weeks younger than Aliyah. Luckily she had enough aunts and grandmothers to keep her grounded.

"Bae! Me and your babies are hungry!" I yelled across the yard to him. Knowing that if I asked anyone sitting with me would have accommodated the pregnant brat. I saw him hand the apron and utensils over to Lamar and come running in my direction with a juicy burger in his hand. He kneeled before me, "your burger my queen."

"Get up silly."

"As you wish my queen." But as he did, he put the burger on the table and pulled me in for yet another kiss.

"Y'all need a room." I heard one of my sisters yell.

"We'll be right back." He called over his shoulder as he scooped me up and led me inside.

CPSIA information can be obtained
at www.ICGtesting.com
Printed in the USA
LVHW041028240223
740259LV00005B/464